Don and Vicki,
Co-Rulers of Oz

Don and Vicki, Co-Rulers of Oz

James L Fuller

Founded on and continuing the famous Oz stories by L. Frank Baum

iUniverse, Inc.
New York   Bloomington

Don and Vicki, Co-Rulers of Oz

iUniverse books may be ordered through booksellers or by contacting:

iUniverse
1663 Liberty Drive
Bloomington, IN 47403
www.iuniverse.com
1-800-Authors (1-800-288-4677)

ISBN: 978-1-4502-0346-3 (sc)
ISBN: 978-1-4502-0347-0 (ebk)

Fuller Publishing
1059 Salmon Ave.
Coos Bay, Oregon 97420
541-888-2857
E-mail: jamesleonfuller@yahoo.com

Printed in the United States of America

iUniverse rev. date: 1/06/2009

Acknowledgments

I wish to acknowledge that my drawings of the Tin Woodman, Scarecrow, the Wizard of Oz, Winged Monkeys, the Emerald City, and Glinda's Girl Guards are based on drawings by W. W. Denslow.

I wish to acknowledge that my drawings of Button Bright, Glinda, the Shaggy Man, the Shaggy Man with donkey head, the Shaggy Man in the Truth Pond, Button Bright with fox head, Great Book of Records, Big Lavender Bear, Little Pink Bear, the Hungry Tiger, Ozma, Professor Wogglebug, Prince Pumper, and the Tin Castle are based on drawings by John R. Neill.

I wish to thank my wife, Ellen, for putting up with all my ideas for this book, and encouraging me. I also thank my sister, Betty Fuller for reading through the book and finding many of my little errors.

Contents

Acknowledgments v

Chapter 1 Going for the Record...1

Chapter 2 The Flight Begins 6

Chapter 3 Robert Seeks Help 18

Chapter 4 An Unexpected Detour..21

Chapter 5 The New Rulers Get Settled 32

Chapter 6 The New Rulers Hold Court 41

Chapter 7 King Dox and King Kik-a-Bray Honor the Rulers..........46

Chapter 8 Button-Bright and the Shaggy Man are consulted..........51

Chapter 9 A Trip to the Truth Pond..56

Chapter 10 A Quick Tour of Winkie Country.....................................60

Chapter 11 A Visit to Gillikin Country 65

Chapter 12 Welcome to Munchkin Country..70

Chapter 13 Sight Seeing in Quadling Country 76

Chapter 14 A Magic Council is Held..80

Chapter 15 The Magic Mirror is consulted..83

Chapter 16 The Little Pink Bear is consulted.......................................86

Chapter 17 Glinda Explains the Picture and Bear's Answers 89

Chapter 18 The Source of the Spell Uncovered 91

Chapter 19 Ozma and the Others Are Released From Spell..............95

Chapter 20 Vicki and Don Abdicate Their Thrones 102

Chapter 21 The Wizard Helps Test Drive the Balloon....................108

Chapter 22 Returning to the Outside World....................................111

Chapter 23 The Balloon is found 115

Chapter 24 The Balloon Flight Continues 121

Afterward 123

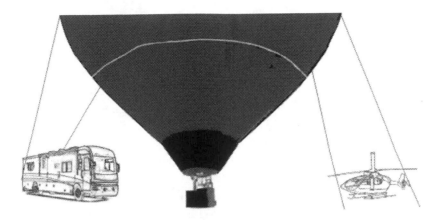

Chapter 1

Going for the Record

It was three o'clock in the morning. The day was June 20, the next to the longest day of the year. The ground crew helped Vicki and Don to climb inside a basket hung below a huge hot-air balloon. They wanted to inspect its contents one more time before they start on their record flight. The basket was five feet square with four feet high sides.

"Don and Vicki, what are you doing? You children come away from there right now! You don't want to break anything," called Peggy Black.

"We won't break anything, Auntie Peggy!" Don assured her. "We can hardly be called children. It will not be long until we will be going away to college."

"That's right, Mother! We know what we're doing," added Vicki. "How many other 'children' of our age have already earned hot-air balloon pilot licenses?"

"Okay, I guess I will admit that you two children are very mature for your age," responded Peggy. "I just want everything to work right when you go for the North America Trans-Continental hot-air balloon record. It is still very early in the morning. Don't you think you should still be in bed? You won't be taking off until six o'clock."

"We couldn't sleep," stated Don. "I guess we're just too excited about the balloon trip."

"You best come back to bed and try to rest for at least a couple more hours," insisted Peggy. "Come on back inside."

"We're coming," called Vicki and Don in unison, as they were helped out of the basket and walked back to the large recreational vehicle that was parked nearby.

The balloon and vehicle were parked at the west end of the Aquatic Family Amazement Park's parking lot in Mission Bay, California. They were using the recreational vehicle as their headquarters for launching their try for the balloon record. Vicki and Don were trying to set a new record for flying a hot-air balloon across the United States from San Diego, California to New York, New York. They were trying to set records for both the time required for the trip and for the youngest balloon pilots ever to make the trip. The record was held by Malcolm Forbes who flew a hot-air balloon from Sunset Beach near Charleston, Oregon to the Chesapeake Bay near New Port News, Virginia in 32 days in 1973.

As Don and Vicki reached the door to the recreational vehicle, they turned and took one more look at the balloon sitting in the parking lot. The balloon was lit up by a hundred bright spot lights. It was a huge black balloon with a large black basket under it. The balloon was tugging at the ropes that held it to the ground. Reluctantly, they turned around, entered the vehicle, and laid down on two of the several beds available in the vehicle. In a few minutes, they were trying to sleep once more.

The balloon was designed by Robert Black, who was Vicki's father, Don's uncle, and Peggy's husband. He used the latest materials in making the balloon. The balloon's bag was made from metalized Mylar for strength and lightness. It was very large and held 750,000 cubic feet of air. The outer layer of the bag was treated with a new heat absorbing coating, colored black. This layer could be remotely turned over to reveal a silver heat reflecting surface. It was rumored that this heat absorbing coating would allow the hot-air balloon to stay aloft using just the energy absorbed from the light of a full moon.

The basket of the balloon was constructed out of carbon composites to give it great strength with little weight. It was five foot square with sides four foot high. Since the balloon was expected to fly from sun up to sun down, one corner of the basket was taken up by an ultra-lightweight chemical toilet. This was enclosed in a two foot by three foot space with a cover over this part of the basket. The rest of the basket was uncovered. There were two fold down seats, an ice chest, a compact radio transceiver, and some storage containers in the rest of the basket. It left little room for moving around. There was a propane burner hung between the basket and the bag. It connected to a small titanium fuel tank filled with propane. This could be used to control the balloon's descent. Using titanium saved half the weight of the more normal steel tank. There was a titanium oxygen tank below one of the folding seats. A coil of rope and titanium anchor hung on the outside of the basket.

With the heat absorbent material now showing on the outside of the bag, the energy absorbed from the hundred spotlights was enough to lift the balloon off the ground and have it tugging at its securing lines. Earlier in the day, the ground crew had used a large portable propane tank to run the propane burner while the balloon was being inflated. This had now been removed and the spotlights were keeping the air in the balloon hot enough to lift the balloon off the parking lot.

By five-thirty, Don and Vicki were up, dressed, had eaten breakfast, and were once more outside looking over the balloon and its equipment. Peggy and Robert were with them. Here at sea-level, it was a cool, windless morning around sixty degrees Fahrenheit. There wasn't a cloud in the sky. Two local television stations had sent news teams to cover the takeoff of the balloon. An early morning radio talk show host was there conducting his show live from the balloon launching. There were a few other curious spectators along with a four-person ground crew for the balloon. They had helped Robert set up the hot-air balloon.

The two news crews asked Vicki and Don for a brief interview. Robert agreed for them to have five minutes of time.

The two stations set up their cameras and the reporters introduced Don and Vicki to their audiences.

"Don and Vicki, why do you want to make this balloon flight?" asked the first reporter.

"Because we like to fly balloons," stated Vicki. "It's fun!"

"You are just doing this for fun?" questioned the second reporter.

"It is fun all right," added Don, "but I think it will be even more fun to set a new world record."

"That's right," recalled Vicki. "Don and I are trying to set a new record for flying a hot air balloon from here to New York. We will also be the youngest pilots to try and do this flight."

"You do seem young for such a feat," remarked the first reporter. "Do you have to have any special training to do this flight?"

"Well, the Federal Aviation Agency (FAA) does require one to get a balloon pilot license," stated Don . . .

* * *

Once the interview was over, Robert reviewed all the trip plans with Don and Vicki one more time.

"You two understand that you won't be alone up there, don't you?" requested Robert.

"Yes, Uncle Robert, we understand that," replied Don. "You have arranged that you or someone else will keep an eye on us from an airplane or helicopter all the way to New York City. It was the only way you could get the Federal Aviation Agency to agree for Vicki and me to make the trip without a more experienced pilot."

"And we will be able to talk with our watchers by radio," commented Vicki. "I just hope all the observers will not disqualify us for the records."

"Don't worry about that. You will be able to set the record if you successfully make the flight," stated Peggy. "I wish I was going with you. I know I will be worried sick until I am told that you have reached New York safely."

"We have already talked about that, dear," replied Robert. "The children will be just as safe in the balloon as they would be at home. You know your added weight to the balloon would make the trip less likely to succeed."

"I know. I know! But I just can't help but worry about the children," cried Peggy.

"It will all be over in a couple of weeks," announced Don. "Afterwards, I know you will be proud of us for setting the new records. You'll just remember how easily it was done."

Peggy remarked, "I have always been proud of you three! It doesn't take a record by you to make me proud of you."

"It is time to get ready," announced Robert. "You can see the dawn's light in the east. Get in the basket and checkout all your equipment. You only have fifteen minutes until sunrise."

Don and Vicki were helped into the basket. Even with their added weight, the balloon was still pulling at its ropes.

Vicki flipped a switch and spoke into a compact radio. "This is Balloon One. Do you hear me, Shadow One?"

An answer came from the radio, "This is Shadow One. We hear you loud and clear."

Shadow One was the helicopter that would watch over them for the first part of the flight. It was parked at the east end of the Aquatic Family Amusement Park's parking lot.

"Are you sure you have all your equipment and supplies?" asked Robert.

"Yes, everything is here!" said Don. "We have checked and double checked everything, several times. We also have maps and the latest weather forecast with us."

"Well, it sounds like you are ready for your departure," announced Robert.

"So, just untie the ropes and we can be on our way," requested Vicki.

"Not for a few more minutes," warned Robert. "You have enough energy from the spotlights to lift the balloon, but there isn't enough sunlight yet. You would just fall back to the earth within a minute or two."

"Well, we could use the propane burner to get high enough for the sun to reach us," suggested Vicki.

"Just save the propane for emergencies and for help in crossing the mountains," said Robert. "You will get to leave soon enough. I'll call you on the radio when the conditions are right. Goodbye for now."

"Talk to you later!" called Vicki and Don after Robert.

Robert was already on his way to the helicopter. He reached it several minutes later. Meanwhile, the talk show host came over and talked to Don and Vicki and had them say hello to his audience. By the time he finished talking with Vicki and Don, the edge of the sun could be seen peaking over the horizon.

"Well, Vicki, are you ready for this flight?" asked Don.

"I am as ready as I can ever be, Don," responded Vicki. "It shouldn't be long now."

"Balloon One, this is Shadow One," crackled the radio.

"Balloon One here," replied Don.

"Don and Vicki, this is Robert. We are taking off and going up to three hundred feet and see how things look," announced the radio. "If everything is okay, we will call you and let you takeoff."

"We will be awaiting your call," stated Vicki into the radio.

Don and Vicki could hear the helicopter start its engine. It warmed up the engine for several minutes. This was followed by an increase in noise level, and the helicopter took off and started gaining altitude. It was also moving away from them so that its winds would not influence the balloon's flight. The plan called for the helicopter or airplane watching the balloon to stay at least one-half mile away from the balloon.

The noise from the helicopter died out as the helicopter got further away from the balloon. Meanwhile, Vicki and Don could see that half of the sun was now above the horizon.

The next several minutes seemed to hang like an eternity, as they waited for the signal to launch. If the flight would just get started, it would make them feel so much better. Waiting was nerve racking! Even the ground crew was anxious to get the flight under way. Weeks of planning and building had gone into preparing for this flight. Would it never begin?

Chapter 2

The Flight Begins

Finally, the waiting ended with the radio crackling to life. "Vicki and Don, this is Robert. Everything looks good. Tell the ground crew to launch the balloon."

"Okay, fellows," shouted Don, to the ground crew, "launch the balloon!"

Three men and a woman untied the four securing ropes holding the balloon to the earth. The Balloon rose slowly into the morning sky, trailing the ropes below it. Don and Vicki waved at Peggy and the ground crew. The ground crew and Peggy returned the wave. Television cameras followed the liftoff of the balloon. The radio talk show host described the liftoff to his listeners.

Everyone was very nervous for the next few minutes as the balloon continued to rise. Vicki and Don were too excited to breathe normally. They watched as the parking lot became smaller and smaller. Vicki and Don could see how close they were to the ocean. Next, they got a good view of all of the Aquatic Family Amazement Park. By now, they were well above all of the electrical power lines in the nearby area. Many balloon accidents have involved encounters with electrical power lines.

As the balloon passed three hundred feet in altitude, it caught up with the helicopter. The helicopter and balloon continued to rise together.

Finally, after Don and Vicki could see the whole sun above the horizon, they relaxed and started to breathe normally again. The balloon was already five hundred feet in the air! Don and Vicki could see most of Mission Bay.

"How high are we going to go before we try to stop rising?" asked Vicki.

"We want to catch a wind that will blow us to the east," stated Don. "The weather forecast predicts there are such winds around five thousand feet. It will be cooler at that altitude. We better put on our flight suits."

"That's a good idea," agreed Vicki.

She got out her black fur-lined flight suit and started putting it on. Don found a similar flight suit for himself and got into it. They wrapped long white aviator scarves around their necks. The flight suits include fur-lined boots, gloves, and a tall turned up collar which could be attached to a helmet and faceplate. The suits were designed to keep the balloonist warm up to twenty thousand feet. This balloon trip shouldn't go higher than fifteen thousand feet.

"Perhaps we should tell Shadow One our plans for looking for a wind to blow us toward the east," suggested Don.

"Let me do it," requested Vicki. She flipped a switch and talked into the radio. "Shadow One. This is Balloon One, over."

"Balloon One, this is Shadow One. Go ahead. Over," spoke a voice from the radio.

"We are now at … What is our altitude, Don?" asked Vicki.

"We are at seven hundred feet," replied Don.

"We are at seven hundred feet and rising," stated Vicki. "We are looking for a wind to blow us toward the east. The weather forecast said there might be such winds at around five thousand feet. Right now, we appear to be moving slowly northward, over."

"That sounds good. Let us know when you find your wind. Over and out!" spoke the radio.

"This is Balloon One, out!" answered Vicki.

"So far, things seem to be going well," remarked Don. "Even a little wind headed north won't hurt us. We do need to travel north as well as going very far to the east."

"That's true," agreed Vicki. "Now, just keep an eye on the compass so we will know when we have found our wind. However, you are right about things going well. And could you ask for a nicer day for a balloon trip? What a view!"

"Yes it is! We can see for over one-hundred miles!" exclaimed Don. "See! There is the ocean on our west and also far to the south of us. I can still make out the Aquatic Park. See, south of the Aquatic Park is the San Diego airport. East of us are the rolling hills and houses of San Diego."

"I see some lakes further east," announced Vicki. "There are mountains much further east of us."

"Those aren't lakes. They are water reservoirs," stated Don. "The first set of mountains to our east is in the Cleveland National Forest."

For the next twenty minutes, the two of them enjoyed the view as the balloon rose steadily higher. At twenty-five hundred feet, they found a wind that blew them to the east

"Shadow One, we think we have our wind at twenty-five hundred feet," announced Don into the radio before Vicki could grab it. "We are going to trim the balloon and stay at this altitude."

Robert's answer came over the radio, "Very good, Balloon One. We will pace you and let you know what your ground speed is."

"Thank you, Shadow One," shouted Vicki into the radio before Don could reply to the message. "Over and out for now."

Don and Vicki got busy adjusting the absorbing surface on the balloon bag. After several minutes, they were able to hold an altitude of two-thousand five-hundred and fifty feet. The balloon now appeared to have black and silver stripes and was moving steadily east.

"Balloon One, this is Shadow One," said the radio. "You seem to have found a twenty-two knot wind heading east. Since a nautical mile is 6,000 feet and a statue or a land mile is 5280 feet, it means you are traveling at about twenty-five miles per hour. At this rate it will take you approximately ninety-seven and one-fourth hours of flight time to travel the two thousand four hundred thirty-two air miles to New York."

"Thank you Shadow One. It is nice to have the trip underway," replied Don into the radio.

"We can only stay with you for another hour," announced the radio. "We have arranged for an old biplane to take over as Shadow Two. Are you having any problems so far?"

"Everything looks great!" answered Vicki to the radio. "Daddy, will you be on Shadow Two?"

"No, I won't be on Shadow Two," replied Robert. "They will take over watching you before we leave you. You will see me again along the way. I hope to be on Shadow Three and some of the other Shadows."

"I wish you and Shadow One could just stay with us all the way," stated Vicki.

"Now, you know that isn't practical," replied Robert. "The helicopter is only good for a few hours of flying time at sea level. It was very handy for following your ascent and can hover to stay with you. However, a helicopter isn't good for high altitudes. It uses too much fuel just trying to stay up high. Fixed wing airplanes work better at higher altitudes then helicopters, but they can't hover to stay with your zero air speed balloon! They have to fly circles around you. That becomes very tiring after a while! So, I have arranged for the Shadow aircrafts to be changed every few hours."

"We will be looking for you on Shadow Three, Uncle Robert," said Don. "Let us know when Shadow Two arrives. Meanwhile, we will keep an eye on our course and look at the great view of San Diego and the surrounding area. This is Balloon One out."

For the next forty-five minutes, the balloon continued to travel eastwardly. The balloon traveled directly over the San Diego zoo. It was still early and the zoo wasn't open. Most of the animals were still in their shelters sleeping. Next, the balloon pasted over rolling hills covered with houses. Every third house seemed to have an outdoor swimming pool. Looking down from the balloon made everything seem like they were miniature model houses with tiny toy cars. The balloon continued moving east past the cities of Lemon Grove and Spring Valley, with the Sweetwater Reservoir just south of it. The houses were further apart now and the foothills of the Cleveland National Forest were growing closer to them by the minute.

The sun was slowly warming up the ground below as well as the air and balloon. The sun caused the balloon's heat absorbing material to warm up faster than the surrounding air, and the balloon rose another hundred feet. Since the wind direction seemed to be staying with the rising balloon, Don and Vicki didn't bother adjusting the trim of the balloon.

"Shadow One. This is Shadow Two. I have the balloon in sight. Where are you?" crackled the radio.

"Shadow Two. We are about one mile north of the balloon at the same altitude."

"That is a Roger, Shadow One. Look for a bright yellow biplane coming up from under you."

"Roger, Shadow Two. Balloon One, do you see Shadow Two yet?"

"Shadow One, there seems to be a bright yellow spot coming up under you," stated Vicki into the radio. "That should be Shadow Two. I guess this means you will be leaving us now, Daddy, doesn't it?"

"If Shadow Two is ready to take over, then I guess this is goodbye for now, Vicki and Don,"

"This is Bud in Shadow Two. I can copy Balloon One fine and am ready to take over for Shadow One. I have Fran with me. She'll keep an eye on the balloon using binoculars."

Vicki and Don called into the radio, "Hello, Bud and Fran!"

"Goodbye, Daddy."

"So long Uncle Robert."

"Hello, Vicki and Don," came a woman's voice from the radio. "This is Fran. Bud and I will take really good care of you two."

"Goodbye Don and Vicki," added Robert's voice. "This is Shadow One leaving. I hope to see you in a few hours when Shadow Three comes on duty. Be careful. You are just entering your first mountains."

"We'll be careful, Daddy," promised Vicki.

The radio became silent. Vicki and Don saw the helicopter turn back toward San Diego. Suddenly, they felt like they were all alone. Of course they could see Shadow Two slowly circling around them, but it just wasn't like having a Father or Uncle watching over them.

During the next hour, the balloon was flying over a forest of live oak trees and scrub brush. It flew between mountain peaks that reached as high as 3,400 ft. By now the balloon was up to twenty-seven hundred feet and had no trouble riding the wind through the mountain passes which were only two-thousand feet high.

The mountains were followed by the Anza-Borrego Desert State Park. This was barren desert that slowly sloped back down to sea level and a little below. The balloon was too high for Don and Vicki to make out many details about what was below them.

The day was warming up, and the balloon had drifted up to three thousand feet. The wind was still blowing to the east or possibly a little north of east which was even better for their purposes. Don and Vicki watched the scenery go by, ate a little snack, and drank a little water.

They were now more than three hours into the flight to New York. Being young, they were beginning to grow a little bored by how long the flight was taking. After all, it didn't take much work to keep the balloon on course.

"We should have thought of bringing some games with us," suggested a tired Vicki.

"That would have added unnecessary weight to the balloon," stated Don. "We can use some mind games, such as twenty questions to pass the time. We might even tell each other some stories."

"That's a good idea! Why didn't I think of that?" replied Vicki.

"Because I am the older member of this crew," announced Don, "and have more experience."

"Oh, come off it! I am as bright as you, even if you are two months older than me!" stated Vicki. "Next, you will be telling me you are in charge because you are a man and I am just a woman."

"Well, since you brought it up. That isn't true!" stated Don. "We agreed that this is a joint venture and neither of us is in charge of the other."

"That's right!" remembered Vicki. "Two heads can think of more things than one head can."

"What kind of story would you like me to tell you?" asked Don.

Vicki suggested, "How about a travel story? Do you know any balloon traveling stories?"

"Well, let me think," remarked Don. "I believe the story 'Around the World in Eighty Days,' has a balloon flight in it. So does the story, 'The Wizard of Oz'."

"Those sound like good stories," agreed Vicki. "Why don't you tell them to me?"

"Okay, the first story starts in London, in . . ."

Vicki and Don continued telling stories for over an hour. They only take time out to get a glimpse or two of the Salton Sea as they approached and crossed it. The sea was at an elevation of minus 235 feet and was the lowest point in the United States. This was followed by flying over the Chocolate Maintain Gunnery Range. Fortunately, Robert had foreseen the possibility of this happening and had permission for the balloon to travel over the gunnery range. These mountains weren't very high, but they really did look like chocolate compared to the arid landscape around them.

As the balloon approached the gunnery range, Vicki thought she heard a distant pop. Before she could say anything to Don, the pop was followed by a BOOM about two miles south of them. She knew where the boom originated because she could see the black clouds left by it.

"Don, I think they are shooting at us!" shouted Vicki.

"Don't be silly. If they were shooting at us, they would have hit us," Don assured her.

The booms continued in groups of threes for over a minute, although it seemed much longer.

Finally, Don used the radio, "Shadow Two, what was all that shooting about?"

"Oh, did you hear it too?" replied Fran.

"How could we miss it?" asked Vicki. "At first I thought they were shooting at us."

"You two were being honored by the gunnery range," stated Bud. "What was it, about fifteen shots?"

"I'm not sure, but I think I count around twenty shots," responded Don.

"I doubt that," stated Bud. "All gun salutes are an odd number of shots. So, it must have been nineteen or twenty-one shots you heard. Of course twenty-one shots are reserved for heads of state such as a ruler of some country. You two aren't rulers of a country are you?"

"Not that I know of," answered Vicki. "Cousin Don, are you a ruler?"

"Don't be silly. Who would make me a ruler?" replied Don.

"In that case, I guess we heard only nineteen shots," concluded Vicki.

"I don't know about that. I think I counted seven groups of three shots each," commented Fran. "That would be twenty-one shots. How do you new rulers wish to be addressed? Will that be Madam and Mr. Presidents or just Your Majesties?"

"We are not rulers!" insisted Vicki.

"Perhaps they were just trying to make us feel important," announced Don. "However many shots were fired, it was still a nice jester. This is Balloon One out."

The gunnery range remained quiet for the rest of the balloon's passing over it. Vicki and Don went back to telling each other more stories. Another hour passed.

Finally, the radio interrupted the story telling. "Shadow Two. This is Shadow Three. We see you and the balloon."

"Daddy, is that you! Where are you? It's so nice to hear your voice again," called Vicki into the radio.

"Yes, it's me!" crackled the radio. "I am in the old blue and white twin engine plane coming up under Shadow Two. With luck, I will be with you all the way to Arizona and maybe half way through it."

"It is nice to hear from you again, Uncle Robert," responded Don to the radio.

"Shadow Three, this is Shadow Two," squawked the radio. "If you are ready to take over, I will say goodbye and take my leave."

"That's a Roger, Shadow Two. This is Shadow Three taking over."

Vicki and Don waved goodbye to the yellow biplane as it turned and headed back home.

The biplane wiggled its wings as a goodbye signal.

Another message came over the radio, "Balloon One, I see you have gained some altitude. Did you do it on purpose?"

"The wind currents and balloon seem to be slowly gaining altitude," answered Don into the radio. "It isn't that high, and if anything we are heading a little north of east, over."

"I see that you haven't re-trimmed the balloon. You are at thirty-three hundred feet and still rising and you still have half of the heat absorbing material covered," stated Robert from the radio. "That is amazing!"

For the next hour and one-half, the balloon traveled over a desert which gradually slopped up in elevation. They passed over the city of Blythe, California, which had the number Ten Interstate highway passing through it. They saw itty-bitty cars and trucks on the interstate. A few minutes more and they reached the Arizona-California border. This was marked by the Colorado River. It was nice to see the river of fresh brown water after all the dry desert and the saltwater Salton Sea. It was noon and Vicki and Don ate some lunch. He had a peanut-butter and jelly sandwich, some barbecue potato chips, chocolate drink, and some snack cakes. She had a tuna-fish sandwich, some corn puffs, a few carrot sticks, diet cola, and some jell'o.

Within the next hour, they had entered some more mountains. This time it was the Plomosa Mountains, which were dry and desolate, and had peaks up to 3,500 feet. They were grayish-blue in color from the sagebrush that covered them. Occasionally, a tree was seen among the sagebrush. The balloon had climbed to thirty-five hundred feet and had gained a mile or two an hour in ground speed. It was as high as the highest peak in these mountains. Robert assured Don and Vicki that the flight was going very well.

The number Ten Interstate had broken away from under them to the south. The flight continued over the arid mountains for another hour as it approached higher mountains. Shadow Three was replaced by Shadow Four, a silver colored single engine airplane. Robert promised to be on Shadow Five when it took over the watch in a few hours.

For the next three hours, the balloon continued to gain altitude. Even so, the mountains continued to get higher. By mid-afternoon, the balloon was approaching the Tonto National Forest and was traveling at five thousand feet. The mountains in the forest ranged from 1,300 feet to 8,000 feet.

Everyone was hoping the wind would take a route through some of the passes in the mountains. That way the balloon wouldn't have to climb over the high mountain peaks. Fortunately, most winds liked blowing through the mountain passes.

"Balloon One. This is Shadow Five," called the radio. "I am here with Frank, the pilot."

"Go ahead!" replied Don into the radio.

"We are the red twin engine airplane that is taking over for Shadow Four," continued the radio.

"Welcome back, Daddy!" called Vicki into the radio. "It is nice to hear from you again."

"You have picked up more altitude and speed. You are at fifty-one hundred feet and traveling at thirty miles an hour," continued the voice from the radio. "Keep an eye on the altitude. If you get above ten thousand feet, use your oxygen masks. Be alert! The winds in the mountains can cause you to change speed and altitude very quickly."

"We will keep our eyes on the ground and the altimeter," Vicki assured her father by radio.

An hour went by along with several mountains. The balloon was at six thousand feet flying above a mountain pass. The balloon was now well into the Rocky Mountains.

"Balloon One, you will be entering either the Apache Sitgreaves National Forest or the Fort Apache Indian Reservation within the next hour," announced the radio. "The highest peaks there are 11,000 feet. Be prepared to adjust the trim on your balloon at a moment's notice. Don't be afraid to use the propane burner if you need fast lift."

"We will keep an eye on things," Don assured Robert.

"Did you say Fort Apache?" questioned Vicki.

"Yes, I did," responded Robert.

"I thought that was just a movie prop," stated Vicki.

"It is real and it is on the Indian Reservation," Robert assured her. "You might get to land there for the night."

"That sounds like an interesting place to stop at," commented Don. "That flight should take about an hour or two from here."

A few more minutes went by.

"Balloon One, my pilot has just received a weather update," announced Robert from the radio. "I don't like it. There is a chance of thundershowers in the mountains. Maybe we should call it a day and have you land now for the night."

"I thought we wanted to get to the Indian Reservation before we stopped!" replied Don to the radio. "Besides, I don't see any clouds around us. I do see some snow on the taller mountain peaks in front of us."

"I would rather be safe than worry about what we might have done," answered Robert. "Storms can sneak up on you without much warning. Have you noticed your speed or altitude in the last few minutes?"

"I was talking to you, but since you mention it, our altitude is . . . Oh my! It is seven thousand feet," exclaimed Don.

"Your ground speed is up to thirty-five miles an hour," added Robert over the radio. "You seem to be picking up speed and altitude."

"Don, what are those grayish-black things up ahead of us?" asked Vicki and she pointed in that direction.

"Shadow Five, you may be right," announce Don to the radio. "There seem to be storm clouds forming ahead of us. Perhaps we better set this balloon down?"

"No! No!" shouted Vicki into the radio. "We will be to the reservation in an hour or so. It will be easier to land in something with a little less wilderness than what we are over now."

"Don and Vicki, land now!" screamed the radio. "You are gaining altitude too fast! LAND while you CAN! That balloon isn't made for traveling through a THUNDERSTORM!"

"We are landing!" replied Don.

Vicki and Don adjusted the trim of the balloon. At first they did it gradually. However, the balloon continued to rise. In desperation, they trimmed the balloon so that the heat absorbing material was completely covered, making the sides of the balloon all silver in color. They expected this to cause the balloon to drop heavily back to the earth. Much to their surprise, the balloon continued to rise.

"Shadow Five, we can't stop the balloon's rising," shouted Vicki into the radio. "Daddy, what do we do?"

"Stay calm, Vicki," replied her father over the radio. "You may be riding an up draft. Keep an eye on your altitude. It may take a few minutes for the air in the balloon to cool off. Once you are out of the up draft and the balloon cools off, you will fall. Don't be afraid to use your propane burner to slow your descent."

"We will do that," agreed Don over the radio. "I see we are still rising. We are at eighty-five hundred feet."

"We are also approaching those clouds," cried Vicki into the radio.

"If you enter the clouds, we don't dare follow you," called Robert from the radio. "Just watch your altitude. If you go above ten thousand feet, use your oxygen. If you get below six thousand feet and can't see the ground, then use the propane to stay at six thousand feet. We will listen for you on the radio and meet you on the other side of the clouds."

The clouds were beginning to close around the balloon. The last thing Don and Vicki saw outside of the clouds was the red plane banking and going around the cloud.

The air temperature around the balloon dropped quickly once the balloon entered the cloud. The balloon rose through nine thousand feet. All Don and Vicki could see outside of the balloon was the white fog of the cloud.

Don and Vicki put on their fur-lined boots and gloves. Next they put on their helmets. The balloon continued to rise. At ten thousand feet, Vicki and Don put on their face-plates and connected up the oxygen hoses. They also connected up wires from their helmets to the radio. This would allow them to use the radio and talk to each other over an intercom without taking off the face plates and helmets.

It was getting darker inside the clouds. Lightening flashes began appearing. Thunder was heard. The further into the clouds the balloon went the brighter lightening flashes became with deafening thunder claps. Both Don and Vicki were scared by the light and noise. The balloon was still rising and was past eleven thousand feet.

"Shadow Five, this is Balloon One, can you hear me?" called a frightened Don.

"Balloon One this is . . ." hissed the radio. Then there was only static.

"Shadow Five. This is Vicki. Daddy, can you hear me?" cried Vicki.

This time there was nothing but static.

"I'm scared!" announced Vicki.

"Me too!" answered Don. "We're fine so far. We just have to wait out the storm."

"How high are we?" requested Vicki.

"We are at twelve thousand feet. I didn't think this balloon could travel that high without bright sunlight and the help of the propane burner."

"This isn't the way the flight was supposed to go!" cried Vicki. "It was supposed to be so simple."

"I know, but there is nothing we can do but wait it out," commented Don. "We just sit tight and wait."

"But that thunder is so loud!" commented Vicki. "It makes me nervous."

"Try and rest. Maybe you can shut your eyes and sleep?" suggested Don.

"What if we are asleep and the balloon starts to fall?" inquired Vicki.

"I'll set the alarm on the altimeter to sound when we drop below ten thousand feet," replied Don. "That should give us plenty of time to start the propane burner."

"Okay. I'll try to sleep," agreed Vicki.

Vicky and Don shut their eyes, but they didn't think they could sleep with all the thunder. They rested for what seemed like hours and hours. The storm continued. The wind tossed the balloon around. It went up and down, side to side, and swung back and fourth. Both Don and Vicki were worried about becoming air sick. Being scared didn't begin to describe how they felt! It took all their courage just to keep from screaming.

They were not aware of it, but their oxygen supply was exhausted after two hours. The altitude, with its lack of oxygen, soon had them asleep. They slept on and on. The balloon went wherever the storm wished to carry it. While they slept there was no sound from the radio but static, nor did the altimeter alarm go off.

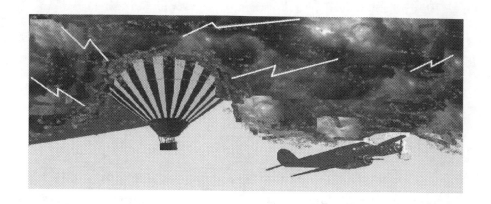

Chapter 3

Robert Seeks Help

Shortly after the balloon with Don and Vicki in it entered the thunderstorm, Uncle Robert lost radio contact with it. Frank turned the plane south to try and fly around the storm clouds.

Robert was worried. He didn't wait to see if the balloon would emerge from the other side of the storm. That could take an hour or more. Immediate action was required.

"Frank," commanded Robert, "set your transponder to squawk an emergency."

Now, setting an aircraft transponder to squawk an emergency causes a message to appear on any air traffic control radar screen covering the air space where the air place is flying.

"Okay, the transponder is reset and I am switching our radio to the emergency frequency," announced Frank. "Now, what do we do?"

"Just hand me the microphone," requested Robert.

"This is Shadow Five to anyone that can hear me," said Robert. "We need help in finding Balloon One, a hot air balloon caught in a thunderstorm around Fort Apache. It was last seen at 7,100 feet and raising. It should show up on radar as a 100 feet diameter sphere or UFO."

"This is Phoenix air traffic control," responded the radio. "Are you reporting a UFO?"

"No! I want to report a lost hot air balloon," replied a frustrated Robert. "It had a ground speed of about forty knots and might be reported as a UFO."

"Don't be silly. Hot air balloons don't show up on radar," stated the controller.

"This one will. Its bag is made from metalized Mylar and it is 100 feet in diameter. It will make a big blip on your radar," insisted Robert.

"If the balloon is in the mountains, our radar will not pick it up," said the controller. "It would have to be at nine or ten thousand feet before radar could get a reflection on it. Hot air balloons don't go that high."

"The record altitude for a hot air balloon is something over 64,000 feet," stated a frustrated Robert. "With the balloon caught in a thunderstorm, it might go above nine or ten thousand feet."

"I don't believe that," replied the still disbelieving controller. "Is this some type of hoax or joke?"

"This is no joke. This is no hoax. This is not drill. You better believe it," insisted Robert. "Hot air balloons can go very high! We have a hot air balloon in trouble. We filled a flight plan for the balloon, Balloon One, and for Shadow Five. Check your records."

Another voice came from the radio, "This is the supervisor of air traffic control, Phoenix. What is this about a UFO?"

"It is not a UFO," answered Robert. "It is a hot air balloon. Balloon One is caught in a thunderstorm and missing. Can you help us find it? You have been told about its flight plan. Have you seen it?"

"Balloon One! Yes we saw that balloon west of us earlier today," stated the supervisor. "It made a huge radar reflection. What is the problem again?"

"The balloon is caught in a thunderstorm near Fort Apache," repeated Robert. "It isn't made for flying through thunderstorms. The storm could damage it. Anyway, we have lost it in the storm. Can you locate it?"

"How long has it been missing?"

"It has been missing for a few minutes or so," replied Robert. "We will try to circle around the storm to the south, but we need you to try and track it while it is in the storm."

"We will let you know if we spot it on radar," announced the supervisor. "Right now the rain in the thunderstorm is so heavy that we can't see anything to the north or west of us."

"We are Shadow Five. Are you tracking us?" requested Robert.

"We tracked you as you turned south," replied the controller. "Now we have lost you in the storm."

"Los Angeles air traffic control, are you tracking Shadow Five?" requested the Phoenix controller.

"We have them," replied Los Angeles controller. "They are still heading south along the edge of the storm. We have just lost Balloon One. We last had it rising through 10,000 feet and moving slowly east."

"Can you guide us south around the storm?" request Robert.

"Yes we can," called the Los Angeles controller. "Continue heading south. We will tell you when to turn east."

"Thank you," answered Robert. "If either of you find Balloon One, please contact us."

"Will do," replied both controllers.

Frank and Robert continued their way around the storm. It seemed like it was taking forever.

Every few minutes Robert was heard calling on the radio, "Balloon One, this is Shadow Five. Can you hear me?"

This was interrupted only once by a message from NORAD, the North American Aerospace Defense Command. They had good news for Robert. NORAD has momentarily spotted the balloon rising through 19,000 feet. Also the thunderstorm was a little one topping out at 22,000 feet rather than the normal 35,000 feet.

What had become of Balloon One? Could it survive such high altitudes?

Chapter 4

An Unexpected Detour

Don and Vicki were still unconscious when the balloon finally started to descend. At first, the balloon lost altitude very slowly. The rate of descent gradually increased.

Within half an hour, the balloon dropped below eleven-thousand feet. Vicki and Don started to wake up. The sun was shining. By the time the balloon dropped below ten-thousand feet, Don was alert enough to hear the alarm from the altimeter.

"Vicki, wake up!" shouted Don. "The balloon is falling!"

"I am awake," replied Vicki. "Let's get the propane burner going."

Don tried to turn on the propane with his gloves on, but couldn't turn the valve. Vicki took her gloves off and opened the valve. It was still cold, so Vicki replaced her gloves.

Don pulled the cord to light the propane burner. The balloon's descent slowed immediately. Another pull on the cord and the descent stopped.

"We are at nine-thousand feet," announced Don.

"Let's try and contact Father," suggested Vicki. She talked into the microphone in her helmet. "Shadow Five. This is Balloon One. Do you hear us?"

There was no answer from the radio.

"Shadow Five, this is Balloon One, over," called Don into his microphone.

Only static was heard from the radio.

"They don't hear us. What should we do?" asked Vicki.

"What do you see below us?" asked Don.

Vicki looked over the edge of the basket in all directions. All she could see below them was sand! It didn't matter where she looked. There was only sand! "We seem to be above a very large field of sand. I wonder where we are."

"We can worry about where we are later. For now this is as good a place as any to land," stated Don. "Let's land and wait for your father to call us. As soon as the balloon cools off a little, it will start descending again. Let's save the propane and try to use the heat absorbent surface to slow our descent. I'll leave the propane value turned on just incase we need it."

"I'll uncover about a quarter of the heat absorbing surface," Vicki remarked as she started working the trim controls for the balloon. The balloon held at nine-thousand feet for several more minutes. Then it started falling slowly once more.

Don and Vicki watched the altimeter to see how much it changed in one minute. It was showing the balloon was descending at twenty-five feet per minute.

"This is a good rate of descent," commented Don. "We want to keep at this rate."

"So, every time it speeds up a little, we just touch the propane burner control," suggested Vicki.

"No! I think we would do better to just adjust the trim to slow the descent," replied Don.

"I knew that," stated Vicki. "If the rate of descent increases, we just uncover some more of the heat absorbing material. If the rate decreases, we just cover up some more of the material. That should be simple enough!"

Vicki and Don watched the altimeter and adjusted the trim for the next hour and one-half. The balloon was now down to fifteen hundred feet. They were so busy with their task that they hadn't bothered to look down at the ground.

Vicki took a moment to stretch and look over the edge of the basket.

"Don, have you looked below us recently?" called Vicki.

"I'm busy!" answered Don.

"I think you better look at this!" exclaimed Vicki. "You really should!"

"Oh! All right!" agreed Don. He looked over the edge of the basket.

"Oh wow!" cried Don. "Where did that come from?"

Instead of the great field of sand being under them, they were now over a very green country next to a city of green buildings! In the distance in every direction were colorful fields of flowers. To the north, the flowers favored the color purple. They didn't know it yet, but they were over the center of the Land of Oz. Back around 1910, by the outside world calendar, Ozma of Oz had ordered the Land of Oz be made invisible from outside of the country. This was done to protect the Land of Oz from invaders. Now that the balloon was about to Land in Oz, Don and Vicki could see it.

"Well, at least we will be close to a city for getting help," commented Don. "Right now, we need to control our landing."

Vicki and Don kept trimming the balloon to control its rate of descent. They didn't notice that a crowd was forming on the ground and was looking up at the falling balloon.

While the balloon was descending out of the sky, a crowd of Oz citizens had been watching it. Nothing like this had happened in Oz since the Wizard of Oz had first come to the Land of Oz more than one hundred years ago and landed at this same spot in the very center of Oz. It was the Wizard who had ordered the building of the nearby city. But this time, the balloon was black with what looked like white strips. White is the color worn by witches in Oz, and black was preferred by wicked witches. Of course this alarmed the Oz citizens.

Among the spectators watching the balloon fall, were the Shaggy Man, Button Bright, the Hungry Tiger, and the Tin Woodman of Oz who was a large, heavy, metal man. Vicki and Don would meet all these celebrities of Oz and more later.

All went well until the last twenty feet. At that point the balloon suddenly dropped like a stone. The impact with the earth knocked Don and Vicki off their feet and down into the bottom of the basket, stunning them.

What happened was that when the tie down ropes of the balloon came within the Tin Woodman's reach, he grabbed one of them and tried to pull the balloon to the ground. He received a large charge of static electricity that made him glow all over with a blue light for a few seconds. Fortunately he was unhurt since he was not made of flesh and blood and couldn't feel the electric shock. However, the people gathered around him were amazed and a little frightened by the glowing.

The Tin Woodman pulled harder on the rope and brought the balloon quickly to the ground just in front of him. When he looked into the black basket, he saw two beings lying on the floor of the basket. These beings were covered from head to toe in black, fur-lined flight suits, with black helmets with dark face-plates, black gloves, and white aviator scarves. The Tin Woodman had never seen people wearing helmets and thought these creatures were very unusual beings.

Vicki and Don looked up from the bottom of the basket to see a strange metal man looking at them. They were scared since they had never seen a tin man before. The large axe on the tin man's shoulder didn't help their being scared. Of course the dark face-plates prevented the Tin Woodman from seeing their faces and their fear.

"Don, what happened?" requested Vicki in a shaky voice.

"We have landed," announced Don.

"I know that, but who or what is he?" asked Vicki.

Since Don and Vicki were still using the intercom in their helmets, the Tin Woodman didn't hear the voices coming from the two beings, but rather from the radio.

"What are you beings?" demanded the Tin Woodman. "Why are you visiting us here in the Land of Oz?" He was so scared that his voice squeaked.

"Well, he seems to be a man made out of metal," Don finally replied, "and he talks!"

"Of course I talk!" responded the Tin Woodman. "Who are you there inside that box? Can these two beings talk?"

"Can't you hear us?" asked Vicki. "I thought you just responded to Don."

"Are there two of you in that box?" asked a puzzled Tin Man, as he continued to talk to the radio. "Is one of you named Don?"

"Oh wow!" exclaimed Vicki. "I forgot that we were still wearing our flight suits and using the intercom. Perhaps we should take the suits off?"

"Perhaps we should!" agreed Don. He took off his gloves and unplugged the wires from his and Vicki's helmets. Don and Vicki removed their face-plates and helmets.

The motion of the two creatures caught the Tin Woodman's attention.

"Now that I can see you two better, I see you are just humans all dressed up!" remarked the Tin Woodman. "But what beings are in that box?" And the Tin Man looked at the radio once more.

"Of course we are humans!" stated Don. "I am Donald Anderson and this is Victoria Black. You may call us Vicki and Don."

"There isn't anyone in that box," stated Vicki. "That box is a radio and an intercom. You just heard our voices as we talked using the intercoms in our helmets."

Vicki and Don took off their boots and unzipped and removed their flight suits. The fur lining of the suits caused each of them to build up a static charge on them. When several of the Oz citizens tried to help Don and Vicki out of the basket, the static charge caused all of them to jump from surprise and pain.

The bewildered Oz citizens thought Don and Vicki were punishing them for touching them. Fear showed on all of their faces. Suddenly, all the Oz citizens bowed down, including the Tin Woodman.

"What are you doing?" questioned Vicki, after Don and she recovered from the electrical shock. "Why are you bowing down to us?"

"All hail the new rulers of the Emerald City!" cried a man in the crowd.

"All hail the new rulers and great sorcerers!" cried the whole crowd as one voice.

Don climbed out of the basket and helped Vicki out of it. Vicki had on black boots, a black and white checkered skirt, and emerald green blouse, and a white belt. Don was wearing black shoes, black and white checkered trousers, a green shirt, and a white belt. Each still had on the white aviator scarves.

"Please! Will you all rise?" requested Don.

"What makes you think we are sorcerers?" added Vicki.

The crowd rose slowly to their feet.

"If it pleases Your Highnesses?" called a woman in the front of the crowd. "All you have to do is look at how you are dressed to know you are either witches or sorcerers. Only witches wear white here in Oz. And black is usually only worn by evil witches."

"We also saw that blue glow you gave to the Tin Woodman and the shock you gave to those who dared touch you," announced the man next to the woman.

"The color green is favored here in the Emerald City of Oz," stated another woman in the crowd. "That's how we know that you must be the new rulers of the Emerald City."

"Where is the Emerald City?" asked Don.

"It is the city right beside us," replied some children. "It is in the very center of the Land of Oz, made up of green colored buildings and decorated with real emeralds."

"Did you say emeralds?" questioned Vicki.

"Why yes! Just look for yourselves. See the decorations in the wall surrounding the city," suggested some more children.

"Don, do you think we could go look at the city?" begged Vicki. She secretly wanted to see if there were emeralds in the Emerald City.

"I guess that will be all right," replied Don. "Perhaps we can get some help from there in re-launching our balloon. Mr. Tin Man. Will our balloon be all right here? We don't want it stolen or damage."

"Your balloon will be fine!" the Tin Woodman assured them. "Several of the men will tie the balloon to the ground so it will not blow away. Come! Let me show you the Emerald City."

Wait!" called Vicki. "What about Daddy calling us on the radio?"

"I will have someone listen for the radio call," said the Tin Woodman. "If you will show them how, they will answer the call and come get you."

"Okay, but we can't stay long. We need to get the balloon back in the air and find my uncle," stated Don.

"That's right! He doesn't know we are safe," agreed Vicki.

Don instructed the men in how to answer the radio call.

"Now, that's taken care of, why don't you follow me and I will show you the Emerald City?" invited the Tin Woodman.

The Tin Woodman started walking the one-hundred yards to the nearest gate of the Emerald City. Don and Vicki followed him. The crowd followed along after Vicki and Don. They walked through a field of green grass.

"Don, where in the world are we?" asked Vicki. "Just look at the people around us, and that live tin man."

Don looked around him. Most of the people were dressed in outfits made from one of five colors: red, blue, yellow, purple, and green. The people dressed in blue were shorter than the others. Don's first thought was these people were all children, but many of them looked too old for children.

"I have no idea where we are," replied a confused Don.

"Perhaps I can help you?" suggested Tin Woodman. "You are now in the center of the Land of Oz, at the Emerald City. To the north of here is Gillikin Country of Oz where people like the color purple. South of us is the country of Quadling of Oz where red is the preferred color. On our east is Munchkin Country that uses the color blue. Finally, to our west is my country, Winkie Country which likes the color yellow. I am its ruler."

"Just before we started to land, all we could see was a great sandy area," remarked Vicki.

"That's right," added Don. "Where did all the sand go?"

"The Land of Oz is surrounded by great impassable deserts," added the Tin Woodman. "The Land of Oz itself is invisible until you are within it."

"Which way is the United States of America?" requested Vicki.

"I believe that is in the outside non-magical world," answered the Tin Woodman. "You are no longer in the outside world. This is the magical fairyland of Oz, which is in the middle of many other fairylands."

"I find all of this hard to believe," stated Don. "This is some type of theme park, isn't it?"

"I'm not sure what a theme park is," responded the Tin Woodman. "However, I am sure they don't have a walking, talking tin man at a theme park."

"Why not?" asked Vicki. "You are just a man wearing a tin suit, aren't you?"

The Tin Woodman halted just short of the city gates.

"I can assure you that I am made of tin and do not have a man inside of me," he announced. "Please, rap me on my side."

Don rapped the tin man on his side several times. He heard an echo to his rapping.

"If you care to open the door on my chest, you can look inside of me," invited the Tin Woodman. "Then you will see that there is nothing inside of me but a red velvet heart filled with sawdust."

Vicki carefully opened the little door on the tin man's chest and peered inside. She saw the red velvet heart and nothing else but empty space.

"I guess that is true," announced Vicki. "You don't have a man inside of you. I am sure people would find your existence hard to believe in the outside world."

Don stated, "If this isn't the outside world, and I haven't agreed to that yet, then how are we going to find my uncle and finish our balloon flight?"

"I don't know!" exclaimed Vicki. "I don't know what we should do. For now, let's just follow the tin man. Maybe he will take us to someone who can help us."

"I guess that's as good a plan as any, for now," agreed Don. "However, if the Tin Woodman doesn't mind, I would like to ask him some questions."

"I don't mind. What are your questions?" replied Nick.

"If this is really the Land of Oz, then where are Dorothy and Toto?" asked Don.

"While you are at it, where are the Scarecrow and the Cowardly Lion?" added Vicki.

"All I can tell you is that Dorothy, Toto, and the Cowardly Lion were in the palace when it was suddenly locked up. The Wizard and Ozma were in the palace too," stated the Tin Woodman. "The Scarecrow, who lives in his giant ear of corn castle in Winkie Country, is taking care of ruling the Winkies until I return. If it would help you believe in Oz, I could have the Scarecrow come visit you."

"I don't think we will be here that long," insisted Don, "but I wouldn't mind meeting the Scarecrow."

"I'll arrange it," remarked the Tin Woodman. He motioned to a nearby Winkie man. The man came closer to the Tin Man and listened while Tin Man gave him directions. Then the Winkie man bowed and left.

The Tin Woodman led the way up to the gate. A gate guardian came out and met the group.

"Who are these two, Nick?" requested the guardian of the Tin Woodman. The Tin Man was once a human by the name of Nick Chopper and still used that name.

"Guardian, this is Witch Vicki and Sorcerer Don. They are the new rulers of the Emerald City," stated the Tin Woodman. "Kindly open the gates for us."

"Right away, Your Highnesses," responded the guardian. "Welcome, Witch Vicki and Sorcerer Don."

"But I am not a witch and Don is not a sorcerer," insisted Vicki.

The guardian requested, "Well, Tin Woodman? What about it?"

"If you had seen them descend from the sky in a black and white balloon, and throw fire at those who dared to touch them, you would believe me," answered the Tin Woodman. "These two are a great witch and a great sorcerer. Just look at how they are dressed!"

The guardian took another look at Don and Vicki. "You are right, Tin Woodman. These are a witch and a sorcerer. Welcome, new rulers of the Emerald City, Don and Vicki!"

Vicki, Don, and the Woodman walked through the gates and into the Emerald City. The crowd followed right behind them.

The Tin Woodman led the way along the main street of the city. It would lead to the palace. There were emerald green buildings on both sides of the street. These buildings had shops on the ground floor. The citizens of the city came out to the street to see who the strangers were.

"Hail Vicki and Don, the new rulers of the Emerald City!" cried the crowd behind Don and Vicki. "Hail the new rulers! Make them welcome in the Emerald City." More people came out of their shops and offered food, drink, and other presents to Vicki and Don.

"I don't like the sound of this," said a scared Vicki. "We are not their new rulers."

"How do you know we are not their new rulers?" asked Don. "Remember the twenty-one gun salute back at the gunnery range?"

"Perhaps you are right!" responded Vicki. "Let's just relax and enjoy looking around the city. Have something to eat and drink."

Both Vicki and Don accepted food and drink from the shopkeepers. Vicki had a nice cool drink of green Emerald City punch along with a red Quadling apple turnover. Don tried some yellow Winkie pastries and drank some blue Munchkin berry punch.

They looked around and saw the many shops they were passing. Of course the street and buildings were all painted emerald green. The buildings were decorated with what looked like huge green emeralds.

"Wow! Will you look at the size of the emeralds used for decorations?" shouted Vicki.

"Those are fake emeralds," insisted Don. "There has never been an emerald the size of one's fist found in the world, right alone with emeralds the size of your head."

"I can assure you that the emeralds used for decorations are all real!" stated the Tin Woodman. "Please try to remember that you are not in the outside world. Emeralds are only used for decoration here. They can be found all over Oz and have no real value."

"Remind me to take some of those worthless emeralds with me when we leave, Don," suggested a wide-eye Vicki. "I am sure I could find a place for them."

"Will you look at that game shop? I bet they have games we have never heard of," announced Don.

"Look at that clothes store, and that hat shop, and the purse shop!" added an excited Vicki. "I hope we get to visit some of these shops."

"There's a magic shop!" pointed Don. "I wish I knew more about magic. After all, I am supposed to be a sorcerer."

"There's a book store. And over there is a pie shop," continued Don. "I think I could learn to like this city."

"You may get to visit the shops later," stated the Tin Woodman. "For now, I am taking you to the palace. You can just see it above the green walls at the end of this street."

Don and Vicki stopped to look at the far end of the street. There was a high wall at its end. Above the wall they could see the many towers of the palace. Of course it was also emerald green.

"If we are going to the palace, are we going to meet the old ruler of this city?" asked Vicki.

"You are going to the palace because you are our new rulers," insisted the Tin Woodman. "Right now, the palace appears to be empty. The old ruler, Ozma, and her wizard, the Wizard of Oz, are gone. They left two weeks ago and haven't been heard of since then."

"What if they suddenly return and find us in the palace?" asked Don. "Wouldn't that cause a problem?"

"They have disappeared. Don't worry about them," replied the Tin Woodman. "I am sure you are to be our new rulers. If and when Ozma and the Wizard return, I am sure we can work out any problems about who is the ruler."

The Tin Woodman and the others turned the corner at the end of the street. They walked to the right along the green wall for several minutes before reaching the entrance gate to the palace grounds. This gate was open and the Tin Woodman led the way into the palace grounds and onto the main entrance to the palace.

The crowd followed along behind until the Tin Woodman, Vicki, and Don mounted the steps leading to the main entrance of the palace proper.

Don and Vicki tried the door of the palace. It was locked. There was a door bell on the right.

"Did you try ringing the door bell?" asked Don.

"Yes we did, but no one answered it," stated the Tin Woodman. "That is why we think the palace is empty."

Vicki tried pressing the door bell. She could hear it ring somewhere inside the palace. She waited a couple of minutes, but no one answered the door.

"There doesn't seem to be anyone home," announced Vicki to no one in particular.

"As I said, Ozma and the Wizard disappeared about two weeks ago," repeated the Tin Woodman. "We found the palace all locked up. All the servants are gone as well."

"Now, what are we expected to do?" inquired Don.

"Why you are a witch and a sorcerer," answered the Tin Woodman. "The key to the palace can be seen hanging just inside the door. All you need to do is use some magic to get the keys. That should be simple for the two of you to do!"

"So, you don't really believe we are a witch and sorcerer," remarked Vicki.

"Oh no, that is I mean oh yes! I believe you are a sorcerer and a witch," replied a scared Tin Man. "It is just that we have tried to get into the palace for two weeks without any success. Surely you can help us get into the palace."

"Why didn't you just break down the front door?" asked Vicki.

"We tried to do that," replied the Tin Woodman, "but the door is unbreakable. We have gone round and round the palace looking for another way in, without any success."

"Too bad you didn't bring along your broom, cousin," remarked Don. "As a witch, you could simply fly up and around the palace until you found someway into the palace."

"I'm sorry I forgot my broom," stated Vicki. "However, as a sorcerer, you could just cast a spell on the keys and have them walk over and unlock the door."

"That's true," agreed Don, "but somehow I don't feel like casting any spells right now."

Unfortunately, neither Vicki nor Don had any magic powers?

What will they do?

Chapter 5

The New Rulers Get Settled

Don and Vicki stood staring at the palace. They were trying to think of some way to unlock the front door.

"Do you agree with me, Vicki, in that I don't feel like doing any enchantments on the keys and you don't want to try flying up to look for another way into the palace?" asked Don.

"Yes, I agree," stated Vicki.

"Have you folks tried walking around the palace looking for another way into it?" inquired Don.

"Yes, we've done that many times without any success," replied the Tin Woodman.

"Do you mind if we do it one more time?" requested Vicki.

"Not at all," answered the Tin Woodman. "Please just follow me."

The group walked back down the palace steps, turned to the right, and started going around the outside of the palace, all the way to the courtyard gate. All the doors and windows on the ground floor were locked. They were made from unbreakable materials

They paused at the gate leading to the courtyard. It was locked. It seems that this gate was controlled by magic. The tour continued on around the palace. The only open door or window they found was a window up on a third floor balcony next to the courtyard. The tour ended back at the palace steps.

"All I saw in the way of open doors or windows was the window in the balcony next to the courtyard," summarized Vicki.

"Let's go back and look at that window," suggested Don. "Of course if someone has a better idea, I am willing to listen to it."

No one had a better idea, so the group returned to the courtyard balcony.

"Have you tried to climb up to that balcony and go in through that open window?" asked Vicki.

"We tried to do that, but the emerald coating on the outside of the palace is too slippery. We just keep sliding back down again," stated the Tim Woodman. "It was also too high for our tallest ladders to reach."

"I think I know how we can get up to that balcony and get in that open window!" announced Don. "However, I will require some equipment from our balloon before I can do it."

"Let me get you a messenger," suggested the Tin Woodman, as he called one of the city's citizens over to him. "Just tell this man what you require."

Don told the citizen to get the rope and anchor that were hung on the outside of the balloon's basket. It took the messenger thirty minutes to go through the city, out to the balloon, and return with the rope and anchor. These he handed to Don with a respectful bow.

"Please don't tell me you are going to try and throw that anchor over the balcony railing?" requested Vicki.

"That is exactly what I am going to do," stated Don.

"Won't that damage the emerald coating?" inquired Vicki.

"Don't worry about the emerald coating," said the Tin Woodman. "It is very strong."

"In that case, everyone move back and give Don some room!" warned Vicki. "Who knows where that anchor may fly?"

The group moved away from Don. Don took hold of the free end of the rope with his left hand. He held the coil of rope in his right hand with the anchor on the outside. Don let the anchor drop down about three feet, and started swinging the anchor back and forth. When he thought he had it swinging through a large enough arc he let go of the anchor and rope in his right hand just as the anchor was reaching the highest point in its swing.

The anchor sailed up through the air uncoiling the rope behind it. The anchor hit the balcony railing and bounced off again. It fell back to earth at Don's feet.

From the back of the crowd the voice of Professor Wogglebug could be heard saying, "You just need to remember basic physics. Let go of the rope when the anchor is at the top if its arch and aimed at the balcony."

Don tried to follow the professor's advice. However, his second throw was worse than his first one.

The Shaggy Man and the Tin Woodman encouraged Don to keep trying and trust his instincts. They also asked the professor to be quiet.

Don tried the throw again, and again, until the anchor finally caught on the balcony railing. He pulled the rope tight and started climbing up the outside wall of the palace. Even though the emerald covered surface was slippery, Don managed to reach the balcony in a couple of minutes. He retrieved the anchor and rope. Don searched the balcony for an open or unlocked door. There wasn't any. He walked over and looked through the opened window. There was a curtain across the window, but no screen. He was able to move the curtain aside and lean inside the window.

Don went back to the edge of the balcony and announced, "I found an open window that I can get into the palace through. I will meet all of you back at the main entrance of the palace."

"We're on our way," responded the Tin Woodman, as he led the way back to the main entrance.

Vicki, the Tin Man, and the others reached the main entrance before Don. A moment or two later, Don arrived at the inside of the entrance. He took the keys off the wall by the door. In another minute, he had found the right key and opened the entrance of the palace.

"Welcome to my palace," announced Don. "Won't you all come on in?"

"You mean to OUR Palace, don't you?" corrected Vicki, as she entered the palace.

She was followed by the Tin Woodman and then by many of the citizens of the Emerald City.

"You are right, Vicki. Let me rephrase my last statement," requested Don. "Welcome, Your Highness, Ruler of the Winkies, and all the citizens of the Emerald City. As your new rulers, Vicki and I request that you make yourself at home in Our Palace."

"Now, that we are in the palace, what should we do?" asked Vicki.

"I think we need to search the palace and see if we can find any clues to what happened to Ozma, the Wizard, and the others," suggested the Tin Woodman. "Come on and follow me."

The Tin Man led the way through the palace. Up and down the passageways went the group. They stopped and peered into each room as they passed it. They went up and down all the stairs, through each floor, up into each tower room, and even down into the cellar.

Not a person or creature was found anywhere in the palace, or the courtyard, or even the royal stables. However, in the kitchen, there were pots of food that had been over cooked on the stove. A sink full of dirty dishes had water overflowing it. There were broken dishes lying on the floor next to the sink. Broken dishes and food were found on the floor between the kitchen and dining room. The dining room table had half-eaten plates of food on it. In the living area of the palace, there were clean towels and sheets on the floor. The beds were half made. All in all, whatever had happened had most likely happened without any warning!

"This is very strange and a little scary," announced Vicki, to no one in particular. "Are you sure it is all right for us to be in the palace?"

"Of course it is all right," stated Don. "We are now the rulers of the Emerald City, and this is our palace."

"His Majesty, Don, is quite right!" agreed the Tin Woodman. "As our new rulers, you are welcome to live in the palace. Let me get some servants to clean up these messes and then we can decide what to do next."

The Tin Woodman bowed to Don and Vicki and turned to talk with some of the Emerald City's citizens. Several of the citizens left on errands.

"May I suggest that we go to the throne room and wait for the servants to prepare your quarters?" recommended the Tin Woodman. He led the way to the throne room without waiting for an answer.

Vicki and Don just walked along behind him. They were very quiet. When they entered the throne room, both of them were surprised at seeing a great emerald throne at the head of the room. It sparkled with green light.

"Wow!" remarked Don, with his eyes fixed on the throne.

"That is so beautiful!" exclaimed Vicki, as she hurried forward to touch it.

"I must apologize for there only being one throne," stated the Tin Woodman. "We have never had two rulers of the Emerald City at the same time before. Of course I will give orders to make another throne, immediately."

"That is very kind of you," replied Don walked up to the throne and stopped beside Vicki.

Don and Vicki climbed the three steps of the throne. There were emerald lions on the ends of each step. Vicki sat down in the seat of the throne. Then she got up and invited Don to try the seat out. Don did this.

Vicki tried to sit down next to Don on the throne seat, but it was too crowded. She then sat on Don's lap, but Don objected to it.

"You are right, Tin Man. It seems we do need another throne," announced Vicki.

"Perhaps not," remarked Don. "Why don't we both just sit side by side on the top step of the throne?"

Vicki and Don tried sitting side by side on the step. It was a foot wider than the throne seat. They fit on the step without any crowding.

"I think we can just use the step until another throne is built," stated Don. "What do we do next?"

"Shouldn't we get help with our balloon?" Vicki reminded him.

"I'm sorry. I forgot about the balloon," replied Don as he tried to image what it would be like to be a ruler. "We really should be going, Tin Woodman."

"It is getting late," answered the Tin Woodman. "Perhaps you should spend the night here at the palace and we can help you with your balloon tomorrow."

"I'm sorry, but we are not prepared to stay here tonight," stated Vicki. "Beside, we didn't bring any clothes or toothbrushes with us. Surely you can't expect us to sleep in and wear these clothes tomorrow, can you?"

"I am sure we can rough it for one night, Vicki," replied Don. "The Tin Man is right in that we don't want to leave this late in the day. Who knows how long it will take to get back to the outside world? Surely, you don't want to travel by balloon at night?"

"No, I don't want to travel by night, but I do want to find Daddy quickly!" answered Vicki. "Oh, all right! I guess we need to stay here in the Emerald City for tonight. So, where do we stay?"

"I will have quarters readied for you," stated the Tin Woodman. "You can have guest quarters or you can have the royal suite. Which would you prefer?"

"I think we are a little new at being rulers," stated Don. "I don't think I would want to stay in the royal suite just yet. Besides, it looked like someone else was already living in there."

"You are right, cousin," added Vicki. "Just show us to some quest quarters. We can explore the royal suite after we are more used to being rulers."

Just then, a group of servants came into the throne room. They talked with the Tin Woodman and then walked up to the throne and bowed to Don and Vicki.

"Your Majesties, we have prepared some quarters for you next to the royal suite," announce the head servant. "If it pleases, Your Majesties, we will take you there now."

"We would be most honored to follow you," answered Vicki, as she and Don got up and walked down the throne steps.

Two servants led the way to the quarters which were indeed next to the royal suite. These quarters were reserved for visiting rulers. Actually, Vicki and Don each got their own quarters with a connecting door between them. Each quarter was really a suite of rooms including a sitting room, a dining room, a bedroom, and a bathroom with a very large bathtub. There were closets in the bedrooms with clothes in just the right size for the quarter's occupant. Of course Vicki's closet had ball gowns, formals, dresses, and tops and bottoms for all occasions. Don's closet had suits, tuxedos, and everyday clothes.

Don and Vicki inspected both of the quarters. It was clear by the clothes as to which quarter was for whom.

After looking in the closets, Vicki was heard to remark, "Well, at least I won't be able to say that I have nothing to wear. In fact, my problem will be in choosing what to wear."

"That's true enough," agreed Don. "I found everything I wanted except for food. There isn't any kitchen. I am getting hungry! Where do we eat? What do we eat?"

"You can eat anything you wish," announced a servant. "If you will just tell us what you want and when you want it, it will be arranged for you. You can eat it right here."

"Wow! Did you hear that? We get room service!" commented Vicki.

"I think I am ready to eat now," announced Don.

"You are always hungry," stated Vicki. "I think we should clean up a little first. Why don't we have a formal dinner for two in my dining room, say in two hours?"

"I don't think I can wait that long," replied Don. "Couldn't you make it in an hour?"

"I'll try," answered Vicki, "but I think it will take me a while to get ready for dinner."

"We could help Your Majesties in getting ready for dinner," suggested a servant. "I am sure we can have you ready in an hour."

"Very good!" remarked Don. "We will have dinner in your dining room in one hour, Vicki. Now, what shall we eat?"

"Why not try out some of the local dishes?" suggested Vicki. "I am sure the cook has some specialty. We will have that."

"If you don't have any more questions, I will see you two in the morning," said Nick and he turned to leave.

"Just one minute, if you please," called Don. "Why don't you join us for dinner?"

"I don't think I should," responded the Tin Man. "Besides, I don't eat. I am sure there will be plenty of time to talk about things over breakfast. You two just enjoy yourself for now."

"Very well, you may go," stated Vicki. "However, please be here for breakfast so we can talk with you."

"I will," replied the Tin Woodman. "By then, I hope to have thought of a plan on what to do. By the way, I'll bring the Scarecrow with me to breakfast."

"Thank you. We would love to meet the Scarecrow," said Don.

Don went to his quarters along with several male servants. The servants showed Don some tuxedos and explained how nice he would look if he would wear one of them. They helped Don to take a quick bath and then to dress up in the tuxedo. When Don looked in the mirror at himself, he was amazed at how matured he looked in the tuxedo.

Meanwhile, some female servants were helping Vicki to bathe, set her hair, and dress her in a white ball gown. She was given a white pearl necklace to wear with white pearl ear rings. The outfit included a white handbag and white high heel shoes. When the servants had finished dressing Vicki, she got to look at herself in the mirror. She could hardly recognize the person staring back at her from the mirror.

"Are you sure that is me?" questioned Vicki.

"Yes Your Majesty! That is really you," replied one of the servants.

"The gown looks great on you!" assured another servant "Don't you like it?"

"Oh yes, I like it!" responded Vicki. "It's just that I have never worn a gown this pretty before."

"You'll get used to pretty clothes after you have been a ruler for a while," stated another servant. "But come, it is time for diner. You should be in your seating room waiting for your cousin."

The servants led the way and took Vicki to the sitting room.

They just had time to get Vicki seated when there was a knock on the connection door to Don's quarters.

One of the servants answered the door and let Don in. The servant announced, "Presenting His Majesty Donald, Co-Ruler of the Emerald City.

Vicki rose and walked toward Don. "Wow. You do look so handsome and grown up in that tuxedo! I never knew you were so good looking"

"Have you looked at yourself, cousin?" responded Don. "You are so beautiful! If you weren't my cousin, I would fall in love with you. What did you do to yourself? You seem taller."

"Men!" announced an amazed Vicki. "You never notice the details about a woman. I am wearing high heels. That is why I look taller."

"You win. I never noticed any details about you being a woman," agreed Don. "I always just thought about you as being one of my favorite cousins whom I have a lot of fun with. I hope this won't interfere with us being friendly cousins?"

"I don't think it will," replied a happy Vicki. "I am having a ball with you right now. Come on; let's see how the food is around this place."

Vicki led Don to her dining room. A table had been set up for two. There were more dishes and silverware than Don had any idea on how to use. At each place were two plates, three bowls, two knifes, three spoons, four forks, a thing that looked like a nut cracker, and a pick.

"What do I ever do with all those forks?" asked Don. "And what is that bowl with very weak soup in it?"

"The forks are for different courses of the meal," stated Vicki. "They will be used from the outside in. The bowl with the weak soup in it is a finger bowl. It is used to clean things off your fingers. I guess we are going to have an interesting meal."

"I just hope it isn't so interesting that I don't enjoy it," remarked a confused Don.

"Relax. I'll help you through it," volunteered Vicki. "Let's eat."

The servants brought in the soup and salad courses. It was a purple Gillikin clam chowder, with blue Munchkin lettuce salad with vegetables from all over Oz, in the colors of blue, green, purple, yellow, and red. There were yellow tomatoes, blue carrots, purple peas, and red onions in the salad.

"Okay, Don, here is your first lesson on formal dinning," stated Vicki. "The large spoon on your right is the soup spoon. Use it to eat your soup. The little fork on the left is the salad fork. Use it to eat your salad. Do you have any questions?"

"No! I think that will get me started," responded Don. "However, I think the color of soup and some of the vegetables are strange."

"I agree," said Vicki. "The color of the food is different. However, it smells so good!"

Once Vicki and Don started eating, they found the food to be very delicious.

Don reached out to pick up an ear of hot Winkie corn dripping with blue Munchkin butter, using his hands.

"What are you doing, Don?" asked Vicki.

"I am going to grab an ear of corn and eat it!" replied Don.

"No, you don't. This is a formal dinner. You don't use your fingers to eat an ear of corn on the cob."

"But I thought the finger bowls were there because we have finger food?" responded Don.

"The finger bowls are for some finger food, but corn isn't the finger food," announced Vicki.

"I don't understand. What do I use?" asked Don.

"You use those tiny little forks with handles. They are called corn handles and are stuck into the ends of the cob," stated Vicki. "Watch me."

Vicki put the corn handles into an ear of corn. Picked it up and started eating it.

Don followed her example.

"So, what is the finger food?" requested Don.

"I think we will find out in a couple of minutes," replied Vicki.

"Does it have something to do with the next utensil that looks like a nutcracker?"

"That would be my guess," agreed Vicki. "It should be interesting."

Just then the servants brought in a tray of Nonestic Ocean crab.

"That looks interesting," stated Don. "I thought maybe we were having some type of nut."

"Those nutcrackers are use to break the shell of the crab legs so you can get at the meat," said Vicki. "You use them like this." Vicki show Don how to crack a crab leg and use a little fork to remove the meat from the shell.

The meal continued through many courses.

Finally dessert was served with a very rich coffee. The dessert was red Quadling apple pie topped with green Emerald City ice cream.

They both had eaten until they thought they would burst. It was a great meal even if Don had to learn how to eat using good manners.

After dinner, both Vicki and Don were tired so they went to bed. They found silk pajamas on their beds. Vicki's bed was very soft just like she liked it. Don's bed was very large and firm exactly as he liked it.

Both slept very well except for a short dream that they each had. In the dream several people called out to them for help. This included a pretty young lady who looked like a teenager, a girl of about seven years old, a short old man, a large lion, and a small dog. There was a large group of people in the background. What could the dream mean? Who were these people and animals?

By the next morning, Don and Vicki had forgotten about the dream.

Chapter 6

The New Rulers Hold Court

Vicki and Don slept until nine o'clock the next morning. Finally, servants woke them up and helped them get dressed in casual clothes.

Vicki met Don in his sitting room.

"Good morning!" greeted a servant.

"What is so good about it?" requested a half awake Don.

"Why it is a nice sunny day in Oz," replied the servant.

"What day is it?" requested Vicki.

"Why it is June 20," replied the servant.

"What? It can't be June 20," stated Don, who was suddenly wide awake. "Yesterday was June 20. This should be June 21."

"I am sorry. Today is also June 20," assured the servant. "Ozma disappeared on June 20, and it has been June 20 ever since."

"It can't be June 20, or Don and I would just be starting our balloon flight," stated Vicki.

"What we do each day, changes, but the calendar is stuck on June 20," insisted the servant. "Today is June 20."

"We'll see about that," answered Vicki. "Don, have you got your watch?"

"Yes, I do," said Don. "It is 9:30 a.m."

"What date does it show?" asked Vicki.

"It says it is June 20," stated Don. "Now, that is strange!"

"Yes it is," agreed Vicki.

Servants invited them to a breakfast bar set up in Don's dining room. On the bar were hot and cold cereal, beacon and eggs, toast, hot cakes, donuts, juice, milk, and many, many other things to choose from. Don and Vicki tried to try out as many different things as they possibly could.

Several minutes later, a knock was heard on the outside door of the quarters. A servant answered the door and let in the Tin Woodman and the Scarecrow. They joined Don and Vicki in the dining room.

"Your Majesties," announced a servant. "My I present Their Majesties the Tin Woodman and the Scarecrow. Scarecrow and Tin Woodman, these are the Joint Rulers of Oz, Vicki and Don."

"I thought we were Joint Rules of the Emerald City," remarked Don.

"Oh Wow! Are you really the Scarecrow that Dorothy met?" exclaimed Vicki. "What a pleasure to meet you."

"Yes, I am," answered the Scarecrow

"Whoever rules the Emerald City rules all of Oz," stated the Tin Man.

"Gentlemen, won't you please join us for breakfast?" requested Don.

"Thank you, but neither of us eats," replied the Tin Woodman. "However, we would like to talk with you while you eat."

"Of course, you can talk with us as we eat," said Vicki. "Please sit down."

The Scarecrow and the Tin Woodman sat next to Don and Vicki.

"Has the balloon been repaired?" continued Vicki. "When can we leave?"

"The balloon is ready. You can leave anytime, but I don't recommend it," stated the Tin Woodman.

"Vicki is right. We should be leaving. Thank you for everything," added Don.

"You are welcome, but you shouldn't leave yet," insisted the Scarecrow.

"Why not?" inquired Don.

"What direction should you take?" asked the Tin Woodman. "How far is it to the United States?"

"What magic will you use to get there" added the Scarecrow. "None of us have any magic that might help you."

"Help us find Ozma and the Wizard. They will know how to get you home," stated the Tin Woodman.

A worried Vicki asked, "Don, you do know which direction to take to get back to the United Stated, don't you?"

"Well we were going east at the time we entered the storm, so," began Don. "I am sorry. No, I really don't know. Maybe we should wait for more help."

"Perhaps we should try being Rulers of Oz for a little longer," concluded Vicki. "You two are rulers in the Land of Oz. Perhaps you can tell us what we need to do as Rules of Oz?"

"Well, you don't have to do much, most of the time," said the Scarecrow. "You just hold court once in a while to solve any problems your citizens have. And you greet visiting rulers, and so forth."

"Mostly, the Land of Oz rules itself," stated the Tin Woodman. "Of course if someone tries to conquer Oz, you will be expected to defend Oz."

"Is someone trying to conquer Oz?" requested Don.

"Well no!" replied the Scarecrow. "The only problem right now is what happened to Ozma and the others who disappeared from the palace two weeks ago."

"And you expect us to solve that mystery?" inquired Vicki.

"We would be most grateful if you would," replied the Tin Woodman. "That is why you were made the Rulers of Oz."

"You knew we were coming and that we should be your new Rulers of Oz," said Vicki. "How is that possible?"

"Glinda sent us a message telling us you would drop in," replied the Scarecrow.

"Who is Glinda?" asked Vicki.

"How do we solve the mystery?" asked Don.

"How you solve it is up to you," stated the Scarecrow.

"You will get to meet Glinda when you hold court this afternoon," added the Tin Woodman. "She may have some ideas on how to help you solve the mystery. Glinda is the Ruler of Quadling Country in the South of Oz."

"What do we do when we hold court?" requested Don.

"You will get to meet many of the rulers from the counties surrounding the Land of Oz, and some of the other rulers in the Land of Oz," said the Scarecrow.

"How should we act toward these rulers?" inquired Vicki

"Treat them as if they are equals," stated the Tin Woodman.

"Whatever you do, be very careful not to insult any of the royal visitors," warned the Scarecrow.

"That means even if they give you strange gifts, just take them and thank them nicely," added the Tin Woodman.

"Okay. We are to be very polite and grateful," summarized Don.

After breakfast, the four of them retired to Don's sitting room.

They discussed how to act like rulers and what had happened to Ozma and the others missing from the palace. While it was known when and who had disappeared, no one had any idea of how they disappeared.

The discussion continued until lunch time.

While Don and Vicki ate a light lunch, the Scarecrow and Tin Woodman went off to prepare things for the afternoon royal court session.

Servants helped Vicki and Don get dressed in royal robes for the court session.

Finally, at two o'clock servants came and took Don and Vicki to the throne room. Pages carried the rulers' trains.

As they entered the throne room, a chamberlain rapped on the floor with his staff and cried, "Announcing Victoria Black and Donald Anderson, Joint Rulers of Oz! All bow!"

"Please rise!" called Vicki as Don and she entered the throne room.

"Hello! Happy to meet you!" called Don to the spectators.

Everyone in the room was looking at Don and Vicki. Vicki and Don looked around the room at all the important people, most of whom were wearing crowns.

At the front of the room were two large emerald thrones. Don and Vicki slowly walked toward the thrones.

"I see they made a second throne," remarked Don. "Since you are on the right, why don't you take the throne on the right and I will take the throne on the left."

"That is a good idea," agreed Vicki.

After several long minutes, Don and Vicki climbed the two thrones, turned to face the audience, bowed, and sat down in the thrones.

The room became very quiet.

The Tin Woodman stepped up to the thrones and bowed. When he straightened up, he said, "Your Majesties, Vicki and Don, I would like to introduce you to Her Highness, Glinda, Ruler of Quadling Country. It is in the South of Oz."

Glinda stepped forward and bowed to Don and Vicki. She was a beautiful lady.

"Vicki and Don, I and all the rulers here in Oz pledge our loyalty to you," stated Glinda.

"Thank you," replied Don and Vicki. They bowed to Glinda.

"There is one thing you two need to do before you meet the rest of those present," continued Glinda. "Would you both please come down here for a moment?"

"I will if Don will," answered a puzzled Vicki.

"Come on," replied Don as he got up and stepped down from the throne. Vicki followed him.

"First I need you two to kneel down and pledge to protect the Land of Oz, its citizens, and to obey all of its laws," announced Glinda in a loud voice so everyone in the room could hear her.

Don and Vicki knelt down and pledged to protect the Land of Oz and its citizens.

The Scarecrow stepped up to Don. The Tin Woodman stepped up to Vicki. They placed emerald crowns on the new rulers' heads.

Glinda asked them to rise.

"You may now return to your thrones as the new Twin Rulers of Oz," announced Glinda.

As Don and Vicki returned to their thrones, the room broke into loud applause.

Glinda then introduced all the rulers to Don and Vicki. Among these rulers were Gaylette - ruler of Gillikin Country, the Queen of the Field Mice, Evardo - King of Ev, King Rinkitink, the Nome King - Kaloko, the Princess of China Country, King of the Winged Monkeys, King Dox of Foxville, King Kik-a-Bray of Dunkiton, Polychrone - Daughter of the Rainbow King, the King of Bear Country, the Little Pink Bear, and many, many more too numerous to list.

There was no way that Vicki and Don could hope to remember all the names of those present.

Finally after several hours, the introductions and court ended.

Don and Vicki were allowed to return to their quarters. They had difficulty believing that they were really the new Twin Rulers of Oz.

Chapter 7

King Dox and King Kik-a-Bray
Honor the Rulers

After the court was dismissed, the Nome King sent a message to Don and Vicki requesting a private audience with them.

Vicki and Don decided to receive him in the throne room.

He requested the return of a decorated belt that Dorothy had borrowed. Vicki and Don ask a servant if they knew of the Nome King's belt. The servant replied that it was in Ozma's quarters. Vicki had it fetched. It was a broad belt, but not that pretty except for the large jewels in it.

Vicki tried the belt on. Even though the belt wasn't pretty, she sensed it might be special. She liked the jewels.

The Nome King said that the belt had ceremonial value to the Nomes. He offered Vicki and Don a large bag of jewels for the return of the belt. Don started to think the King wasn't telling them the whole story about the belt.

Just then, the Tin Woodman and Glinda entered the throne room unannounced. They asked what the Nome King wanted.

Vicki stated, "The Nome King wants to give us a bag of jewels for this old belt. He says the belt is special to the Nomes but of little use to us."

"You don't say!" remarked Glinda. "In that case let him take the belt off of you."

The Nome handed Don the bag of jewels and reached over to unfasten the belt on Vicki. He was thrown across the room and hit the far wall.

"It seems the belt protects the wearer from mischief, whomever the wearer maybe," stated Glinda. "Did he forget to mention that? It is a magic belt!"

When the Nome King had gotten to his feet and approached the throne, Don handed the bag of jewels back to the Nome King.

"Perhaps the Nome King knows something about Ozma's disappearance?" enquired Don.

"No, I do not," responded the Nome. "I just want the Magic Belt back. I do not suppose you will give it to me now?"

"I don't think so," responded Don. "Vicki and I need to know more about it first before making any decisions about it."

"In that case, I will leave, with your permission," said the Nome King.

"Please do leave," answered Vicki.

The Nome King left with the Tin Woodman and Glinda following him.

"Announcing King Dox of Foxville, in the country of the Scoodlers, which is across the Great Sandy Waste from Quadling Country of Oz," said a page.

King Dox was brought into the presence of Don and Vicki.

"What was the Nome King doing here?" asked King Dox.

"He wanted to trade us a large bag of jewels for the belt Vicki is wearing," replied Don.

"You didn't agree to that, did you?" requested Dox.

"No we didn't," stated Vicki. "We told him if he could remove the belt from me, we would accept his offer."

Vicki took off the belt and handed it to Don. He examined the belt.

"Since he was up to no good, the belt protected Her Majesty and threw the Nome King across the room," added Don.

"Well done Your Majesty, Vicki. That was very clever of you," stated the Fox King. "You deserve a reward for cleverness. Therefore I confer upon you the head of a fox!"

Before Vicki or Don could protest, King Dox did the only transformation that he knew and transformed Vicki's head into a fox head.

"Oh my, that is different!" exclaimed Don.

"What's happened?" cried Vicki, as she felt her furry face and whiskers.

"Why you have just been honored by King Dox and now have a fox head," replied Don. "It is quite charming."

"I don't know what to say," stated Vicki. "I really don't deserve this honor. Please, just give me back my own head."

"Oh but you do deserve the honor, Your Majesty," insisted Dox. "Besides, I don't know how to change you back. Once you are used to it, you will see how much better it is than your own head."

"You really must see it," Don told Vicki, while holding back a laugh.

"Thank you, King Dox for honoring me," said Vicki. "Page, please bring me a mirror!"

"While you are waiting for the mirror, may I suggest that you try out your new head," recommended the Fox. "You will quickly see how superior the fox head is to a human head."

"Inhale and tell me what you smell," continued the Fox.

Vicki took a breath and said, "I smell a chicken and something else."

"Indeed! A hen and her chicks, I believe," agreed the Fox.

"Big deal!" stated Don. "So, the kitchen is cooking fried chicken and eggs."

"It is not cooked food I smell," answered Vicki. "It is a live hen and chicks."

"Now, sniff in several directions and tell me which way to the chickens, Your Majesty."

"Why they are that way," announced Vicki, pointing to one corner of the room.

"There is nothing there!" laughed Don.

"But they were there recently," stated King Dox.

"You two are telling me that you can smell where a chicken has been, after this room was filled with people for several hours," said Don. "There wasn't any chicken in the room during that time."

"Let's take a closer sniff," suggested the Fox King.

He, Don, and Vicki walked over the corner of the room. The Fox and Vicki sniffed all around the corner and around the area back from the corner. The smell of the hen and her chicks was very strong in the corner. However, neither Dox nor Vicki could find any trace of a trail of the chickens entering or leaving the corner.

Don and Vicki returned to their thrones. King Dox followed them.

"That is strange that we couldn't find their trail. The smell is so strong that it is like they are still in the room," stated Dox. "Never mind that for now. Let's try out your hearings. What do you hear out in the hall?"

"I hear running steps," announced Vicki. "I wonder who that could be."

"That is probably the page returning with the mirror," replied Dox. "Wait until you see how splendid you look with your new head!"

"I also hear the clop, clop of someone or something approaching," added Vicki. "Now who might that be?"

"That is probably King Kik-a-Bray of Dunkiton," stated the Fox King. "It would be just as well that he does not meet and talk to me."

King Dox said his goodbyes and left.

The page brought in a mirror and gave it to Vicki.

"This is awful!" cried Vicki as she looked at her new head. "What am I to do?"

"For now, you do nothing," laughed Don. "Just accept the honor. Later, we will get Glinda to give you back your old head. Here take the belt back before something else happens to you."

Vicki took the belt.

A page entered and said, "Announcing King Kik-a-Bray of Dunkiton, in the country of the Scoodlers, which is across the Great Sandy Waste from Quadling Country of Oz."

King Kik-a-Bray of Dunkiton was shown in to see Vicki and Don. He bowed to the new rulers.

"Was that King Dox who just left here?" requested the King.

"Yes it was," answered Don. "You seem to be a donkey."

"Of course I am a donkey, and am glad that I am not a fox or a human," replied the donkey. "Oh, I see Her Majesty has been honored by the Fox King."

"You don't know how to undo his handy work, do you?" requested Vicki.

"Sorry, no," responded King Kik-a-Bray. "I see that His Majesty was not honored by the Fox King."

"No, he didn't think I was clever enough to be honored," answered Don. "I didn't argue the point with him."

"That was very wise of you," agreed the donkey. "You were wise and admirable not to encourage him. For that reason, I wish to honor you."

"What? I wouldn't want to put you to any trouble," replied Don.

"It is no trouble at all," answered the King, and before either Vicki or Don knew what had happened, the King said a magic spell.

Instantly, Don's head was replaced by the head of a donkey.

"Oh Don, I love your ears," snickered Vicki. "You have never looked handsomer."

Vicki handed Don the mirror.

"I can't think of words to say how I feel," stuttered Don. He was horrified by the look of his new head.

"No need to thank me," said King Kik-a-Bray. "Now you are wiser and smarter than all the humans and foxes in the world."

"Does this make me the only donkey in Oz?" requested Don.

"I believe it does, Your Majesty," stated the Donkey King. "However, I believe there is a mule called Hank in the palace stables."

"How am I better off with a donkey head instead of a human head?" asked Don.

"For one thing, you don't need to pick and cook your food," announced the donkey.

"Take a deep breath," commanded King Kik-a-Bray. "What do you smell?"

"I smell clover and grass, outside in the courtyard," announced Don. "Come on. Let's go sample it."

Don and King Kik-a-Bray hurried out to the courtyard. Vicki hurried along behind them. Before Vicki could stop Don, he was down on all fours munching on the clover.

"I never knew clover tasted so good!" remarked Don.

"Yes, the palace clover is good," agreed King Kik-a-Bray. "Wait a minute. I think I smell some oats!"

Don sniffed the air and said, "They are over in the stables."

Don, Vicki, and the donkey run over to the stables. There they find sacks of oats. Don poured out some oats into a feeding trough. He and King Kik-a-Bray started eating the oats.

"I smell something in the next stall," announced Don.

"Oh, that is just a mule," replied Kik-a-Bray.

Don and Vicki looked at the next stall. They could smell a mule, but couldn't see anything.

"What creature do I smell over here?" requested Vicki.

Don walked over to Vicki. He sniffed the air.

"I don't know," admitted Don. "What do you think it is, King?"

King Kik-a-Bray came over and sniffed the air.

"We do not want to stay here!" warned the Donkey.

"Why?" asked Vicki.

"What you smell is a lion. A LARGE LION!" announced the Donkey and backed away from the spot.

"But there is no lion here," insisted Don.

"There has been one here," agreed Vicki. "And I cannot find a trail where it ever left here. This is spooky. Let's go back inside."

The three of them went back into the palace. Vicki and Don said goodbye to King Kik-a-Bray and went back to the throne room.

Don and Vicki needed to find help in getting their back their original heads.

They couldn't continue their balloon trip until they did.

Chapter 8

Button-Bright and the Shaggy Man are consulted

Vicki asked a page to find Glinda and request her to come to the throne room.

Several minutes later, Glinda arrived.

"Oh my!" exclaimed Glinda when she saw Vicki and Don. "I was going to ask what I could do for you, but I think I see the answer to that question."

"It seems King Dox and King Kik-a-Bray honored us," stated Vicki.

"I don't suppose you can turn us back into our former selves?" requested Don.

"My magic has never dealt with this type of problem," admitted Glinda. "However, I do recall that Button-Bright once had a fox head from King Dox, and the Shaggy Man once had a donkey head given to him by King Kik-a-Bray."

"Well, do they still have their fox and donkey heads?" requested Vicki.

"No, they don't," stated Glinda. "Somehow they got their normal heads back."

"So, how did they get their normal heads back?" asked Don.

"We had best ask them that," replied Glinda.

"Page, can you find Button-Bright and the Shaggy Man," requested Vicki.

The page left to look for the pair. Several minutes later, the page returned with a nicely dressed man in a very shaggy outfit.

"Your Majesties, how kind of you to see me," said the Shaggy Man, as he bowed before Don and Vicki.

"We understand that you once had a donkey head from King Kik-a-Bray," stated Don.

"Yes, I did," admitted the Shaggy Man. "I was very glad when I managed to get rid of it."

"So, this is not permanent," requested Vicki.

"It need not be," agreed the Shaggy Man.

"And Button-Bright had a fox head," continued Vicki. "Where is Button-Bright?"

"Button-Bright has got himself lost again," stated a page. "He has not been gone for long, so it should not take very long to find him."

A few minutes late, a second page brought in Button-Bright, a boy of about six years of age, dressed in a sailor suit..

Button-Bright took a look at Vicki and Don, and remarked, "Fox, donkey been here." For Button-Bright was a person of few words.

"So, you remember having a fox head," said the Shaggy Man.

"Better than donkey," explained Button-Bright.

"Well maybe you are right," agreed the Shaggy Man. "Nevertheless, do you remember how we got rid of the fox and donkey heads?"

"Truth Pond!" stated Button-Bright.

"So, you do know how to restore our heads," requested Don.

"Oh yes. It is very simple. You just bathe in the Truth Pond!" announced the Shaggy Man.

"What are we waiting for?" asked Vicki. "Take us to the Truth Pond."

"Where is the Truth Pond?" inquired Don.

"The Truth Pond is on the far side of Winkie Country," said Glinda. "We can travel there by wagon in a couple of days."

"When can we start?" requested Vicki.

"How about first thing in the morning?" suggested Glinda.

"Isn't there some faster way to get there?" asked Vicki. "This head just isn't me. Oh how I want to be rid of it."

"Know feeling," commented Button-Bright.

"I could probably use the Nome Magic Belt to transport us there," admitted Glinda. "However, I think it would be better to see some of Oz as you travel there as the new rulers."

"Do Vicki and I have a say in it?" requested Don.

"Can either of you work the Magic Belt?" replied Glinda.

"No," answered Don and Vicki.

"Then I think it would be best to travel there by wagon," stated Glinda, "for you see I haven't actually used the Belt either."

"Do you want to be Glinda's first Magic Belt transportees or can you wait a couple of days to lose the heads?" asked the Shaggy Man.

"I think we can wait a couple of days," admitted Don. "But please don't make us wait any longer than that."

"Okay! I will make arrangements and we can leave early tomorrow morning," Glinda assured the twin rulers.

Vicki and Don retired to their chambers for the rest of the day. The servants brought food that suited their new heads and minds. Sleeping was a little strange. The fox head wasn't too difficult to manage, but the large donkey head proved quite a problem. Somehow they managed to get through the night. Once again they had the dream about a young lady and others calling out to them for help.

The next morning, they got up early, dressed, eat breakfast, and were out in the courtyard waiting for the others to arrive for the start of the trip.

The Tin Woodman, Button-Bright, the Shaggy Man, and Glinda came out to join them on the journey. They were to take an open wagon, with three seats which seated six very comfortably. When the horse arrived, Don and Vicki were shocked. It seemed the wagon horse was to be the Hungry Tiger!

"I am sorry about using the Hungry Tiger for a horse," explained Glinda, "but both Hank the Mule and the Wooden Sawhorse of Oz disappeared with Ozma. This is the best we can do."

"That is one big Tiger!" remarked Vicki. "I hope we will be safe."

"Just so long as the Hungry Tiger isn't hungry for foxes or donkeys," remarked Don.

"Oh, I never eat foxes or donkeys," the Tiger assured them. "What I would really like to eat is a nice juicy fat baby!"

"How could you possibly eat fat babies?" cried Vicki. "That's terrible."

"Oh, I have never eaten a fat baby," replied the Hungry Tiger. "My conscience will not allow me to eat one. However, I think they would taste so good!"

"We are perfectly safe with the Hungry Tiger," Glinda assured everyone. "No wild animal will bother us while the Tiger is with us."

"Where are the reins?" asked Don.

"There are no reins," stated the Tin Man. "All you have to do is just tell the Tiger where to go."

"Tiger," said Glinda, "please take us west to Winkie Country."

"Is that where the Truth Pond is located?" requested Vicki.

"Yes, it is," responded the Tin Man. "It is at the far edge of Winkie Country. We will be able to visit the Scarecrow's Tower and my Tin Castle on the way."

The wagon moved toward the gate of the courtyard. The gate opened by itself and let the wagon pass through it. The gate closed behind them. The Tiger pulled it swiftly through the streets of the Emerald City. People were only too happy to get out of the way of the Hungry Tiger.

At the city gate, the Guardian took one look at the Tiger, Glinda, and the others and waved them through the gate without making them stop. Once through the gate, the Tiger turned the wagon toward Winkie Country. The wagon traveled along for sometime through fields of flowers. The farther the wagon went the more the flowers featured the color yellow.

After awhile, Don took out a pocket compass and checked the direction they were taking.

"Excuse me," announced Don to no one in particular. "But, we seem to be traveling EAST. Isn't Winkie Country to the West?"

"One of the many defenses of the Land of Oz is that east and west are reversed from their normal compass positions," stated Glinda. "It makes it difficult for invaders to find their way around."

Just as they were reaching the edge of the fields of flowers, Vicki spotted a large flock of birds coming toward them.

"What kind of birds are those birds?" asked Vicki, as she pointed up ahead of them.

"Those aren't birds," stated Glinda. "They are Winged Monkeys. They seem to be coming toward us for some reason."

The wagon halted as everyone watched the flock of Monkeys coming nearer.

The Winged Monkeys landed and their leader walked up to the wagon.

"Your Majesties," greeted the King of the Winged Monkeys. "I am glad I caught up with you." He bowed to the Fox Headed Vicki and the Donkey Headed Don.

"What can we do for you?" requested Glinda.

"It is not what you can do for me, but what I can do for you," replied the Monkey King.

"What can you do for us?" asked Vicki.

"I understand Your Majesties would like to lose the fox and donkey heads," stated the King.

"Can you restore our heads?" requested Don.

"No!" admitted the King. "However, I can arrange to fly you to the Truth Pond in about an hour! That is, if you are interested."

"Interested!" exclaimed Vicki. "Oh what a nice creature you are. That would be wonderful!"

"I take that as a yes, you are interested," remarked the Winged Monkey.

"Yes, we are interested!" stated Don. "How soon can you arrange the flight?"

"It would take five or ten minutes to arrange everything," responded the King of the Winged Monkeys.

"If Glinda has no objections, then I believe Don and I would like to accept your offer," announced Vicki. "That offer is for all of us, isn't it?"

"I have no objections," said Glinda.

"In that case Your Majesties, let us proceed," said the King. "And yes, the offer is for all of you including the Hungry Tiger."

Chapter 9

A Trip to the Truth Pond

The Tin Woodman, Button-Bright, the Shaggy Man, Glinda, Don, and Vicki got down from the wagon. The Shaggy Man unhitched the Hungry Tiger.

The Winged Monkey King had some of the Winged Monkeys fly to a nearby forest to collect vines.

They returned and wove the vines into six swings with backs and seatbelts, and two large slings. Four monkeys were assigned to carry each swing and each sling.

Several monkeys helped Glinda into a swing and it was lifted into the air by four winged monkeys. She was quickly followed by Don, Vicki, the Shaggy Man, Button-Bright, and the Tin Man. Finally, eight winged monkeys lifted the two slings carrying the Hungry Tiger. Eight more monkeys used vines to pickup and carry the wagon.

The group headed west by south-west for the Truth Pond. They flew over fields of yellow flowers, then fields of yellow grass and finally over forest of yellows trees.

They passed over Jack Pumpkinhead's large pumpkin house, then by the Scarecrow's Tower. On their left, a river ran over to the Tin Woodman's castle with sun shining off the castle. Forty-five minutes later they flew over the Winkie River. Shortly after that, Vicki spotted a pond off to their left. The Winged Monkeys altered their course for the pond.

They landed at the edge of the Truth Pond next to a warning sign.

It said, "This is the TRUTH POND." The sign also included fine print.

"What do we do now?" requested Vicki.

"Bathe!" stated Button-Bright.

"Your Majesties simply need to bathe in the pond and your heads will return to their normal shape," stated the Shaggy Man.

"I don't know about this," remarked Don. "I seem to have forgotten my bathing suit."

"Don't worry about it," said Glinda. "It is a nice sunny day with a slight breeze. You will soon dry out."

"You just want us to jump into the pond clothes and all?" asked Vicki.

"That is the general idea," answered the Shaggy Man. "That is what Button-Bright and I did."

"Fall," said Button-Bright.

"He says he just leaned over the edge to look at himself and he fell in," translated the Shaggy Man.

"Perhaps if someone were to just accidently push us in," suggested Vicki.

"You are working too hard at it," stated the King of the Winged Monkeys. "Getting people wet is one of our specialties."

The King signaled to several of his monkeys.

Two monkeys picked up Don, carried him out over the center of the pond and dropped him. He made a big splash.

While Vicki was laughing at Don, two more monkeys picked her up and dropped her next to Don.

When Don and Vicki surfaced in the pond, their heads were restored to normal.

Several minutes later a soggy Vicki and Don climbed out the Truth Pond.

"Well, that wasn't so bad," remarked Don. "It sure is nice to have my own small head back."

"Not so bad!" cried Vicki. "Look at my hair! Look at my clothes. I feel like a wet rat."

"True," agreed Don, "but your head looks so much better than the fox head you had."

"I thought you liked that head," stated Vicki.

"It would have looked good on a fox, but I like you better the way you are now," insisted Don.

"You like me better all wet!" replied Vicki.

"Yes. No. That is, I like you better all wet with your own head than I did with you dry with your fox head."

"You like me, do you?" requested Vicki.

"Well, you are my favorite cousin," agreed Don.

"You would like to date me, wouldn't you?" asked Vicki.

"No. I just think of you as my favorite cousin," insisted Don. "I never thought of you as a girl friend."

"You like the clothes I am wearing, except for the water. Right!" said Vicki.

"Okay. The outfits you have worn as a ruler have been very nice," answered Don. "While we are at it, you do like me, don't you."

"Of course I like you. We have fun together," remarked Vicki.

"So, would you like a date with me?" asked Don.

"I never thought about dating you, cousin. It is a bad idea," said Vicki.

"Would you like a boy friend that looked like me?" questioned Don.

"You are my favorite cousin and all that, but I wouldn't want a boy friend just like you," answered Vicki.

"Be careful what you say to each other," cautioned Glinda. "If you swallowed any water, you will have to tell the truth for a while. You did read the fine print on the sign, didn't you?"

Vicki replied, "What fine print? Who would read the fine print? I mean the pond did get rid of my fox head."

"I thought the sign said for always after," remarked Don.

"The sign exaggerated a little," replied Glinda.

"The pond did get rid of my donkey head. That is worth a few side effects," added Don.

"So what is the big deal? So we tell the truth for awhile. Stay out of this!" requested Vicki. "I mean."

"Yes. We know we have to tell the truth," agreed Don. "Vicki didn't mean anything by her last remark."

"Yes, I did!" announced Vicki. "I mean this is our conversation. Stay out of it. Please."

"Okay, I am not usually that impolite," apologized Vicki.

"Vicki and I are only asking questions we would normally be afraid to ask," stated Don. "We really know the answers to the questions, but we were just checking each other out."

"We really are good friends," added Vicki. "And that is the way we plan to keep things."

"So, what do you usually think of what I wear?" asked Vicki.

"I think they are. That is, I . . ." stuttered Don. "Okay. Sometimes I think your outfits are terrible."

"What do you think of my hair do?" requested Don.

Don and Vicki continued to talk for some time.

By the time Vicki and Don were able to say things so as not to hurt each others feelings, they had dried out.

"Well, telling the truth, the whole truth and nothing but the truth could take some getting used to," remarked Vicki.

"I agree," said Don. "I am glad to hear it will were off."

"If you two are done having fun with the truth," suggested Glinda, "perhaps we could get on with your tour of the Land of Oz."

"Just one more question, but this time it is for the King of the Winged Monkeys," requested Vicki.

"What can I do for you, Your Majesties?" requested the King.

"You can tell us what you meant by 'Getting people wet is one of your specialties'," replied Vicki.

"That is simple," stated the Monkey King. "It was back when my father was the King. We were full of mischief. One time Quelala, the then soon to be husband of Gaylette was walking beside the river in a rich costume of pink silk and purple velvet. My father thought it would be interesting to see how the outfit stood up to water, so he had several of the Winged Monkeys pick Quelala up and toss him in the river. It didn't upset Quelala, but it ruined his clothes."

"So, that was funny," suggested Don.

"My father thought so, but Gaylette didn't think so," continued the King. "It resulted in us Monkeys being made slaves for many years."

"It is what you get for having fun at someone else's expense," stated Vicki.

"On the other hand, the King did help us get our own heads back," Don reminded everyone. "In this case King, you did the right thing by dropping us in the pond."

"Now that all of you are friends, may I suggest that we get back to your tour of Oz?" suggested Glinda.

Chapter 10

A Quick Tour of Winkie Country

"I thought the main object of this trip was to get to the Truth Pond and have our heads restored," stated Vicki.

"It was, but now I think you two should see a little of the Land of Oz," insisted Glinda. "While we are at it we can visit with some of the local rulers in Oz and try to form a plan for getting Ozma and the others back."

"How much of Oz are we going to see?" requested Don

"I should think we will visit all four of the Countries that make up the Land of Oz," responded Glinda.

"That could take days," remarked Vicki.

"Yes, it could," agreed Glinda. "But we need to consult with some of the other rulers and their magic. It will not be a long trip if the King of the Monkey will help us out."

"How can I be of service to you?" asked the King.

"I thought we would visit the Tin Castle, the Scarecrow's Tower, Gaylette's Ruby Palace, Dorothy's old house and the beginning of the Yellow Brick Road, the Royal College of Oz, China Country, and my castle in Quadling Country," stated Glinda,

"If you will add the old Wicked Witch's Castle to the tour, I will have my Winged Monkeys fly all of you around Oz," replied the King of the Winged Monkeys.

"Let's start by visiting the Scarecrow's Tower," requested Glinda. "He was the ruler of Oz, after the Wizard left and before Ozma became the ruler."

Once again, the Winged Monkey lifted the party consisting of the Tin Woodman, the Hungry Tiger, Button-Bright, the Shaggy Man, Glinda, Don, Vicki, and wagon, into the air. Fifty-five minutes later, they landed in a field next to the Scarecrow's Tower.

They turned to get a good look at it and were treated to a most unusual yet breathtaking view of an unusual building. The foundation of the house was made from very, very large emeralds. These had been carved to look like the leaves of an ear of corn. The kernels on the ear were made from gold. Each kernel was the size of a window of a house.

They walked up to the tower. The Scarecrow greeted them at the front door. When they stood at the front door and looked up at the huge ear of corn, it seemed even larger than it had from the air! They never imagined anything like it!

"You do have one very unusual home, Scarecrow!" exclaimed Vicki. "Can we look around it?"

"If you will just follow me, I will give you a tour," suggested the Scarecrow.

Upon entering the house, he showed his guests his living room, which was furnished with straw furniture. There were straw rugs on the floor. They all tried out the sofa and chairs and found them very comfortable. The Scarecrow assured everyone that all the straw had been fireproofed.

The Scarecrow led the way up the straw staircase to the second floor. Here they found a dining room where the Scarecrow often entertained guests. It was furnished with straw tables and chairs. There was a kitchen off the dining room where a large lunch was being prepared. The Tin Woodman had insisted that the kitchen used a tin stove that was chrome plated. The sinks, counters, work tables and refrigerator were also tin with chrome plate. The kitchen tables and chairs were made from straw.

"Of course all of you will honor me by having lunch with me," requested the Scarecrow.

"Lunch sounds great!" admitted Vicki.

"I am so hungry that I could eat two horses," stated the Hungry Tiger.

"I have some raw meat for you," the Scarecrow assured him. "We can eat as soon as we finish the tour."

The tour continued to the third and fourth floors where there were guest bedrooms. The Scarecrow didn't require sleep, so he didn't have a bedroom. The fifth floor housed the Scarecrow's office. Here he and the Tin Woodman spent many a night discussing how to rule Winkie Country.

Don and Vicki were very impressed with the tower. They thanked the Scarecrow for the tour and went back downstairs to the dining room.

The Scarecrow was able to furnish food for the whole party including all the Winged Monkeys. The Tin Woodman and Scarecrow didn't require food, but they sat with the others and talked about the problem of Ozma's disappearance. Those who did require food had their full of delicious food.

Although the Scarecrow was alive by magic, he didn't possess any magic to help find Ozma.

No one had any ideas about the cause or cure for the disappearance.

The group went back outside the tower.

"Thank you for the tour of your tower, Scarecrow!" said Don, as he and the others got ready to fly to the Tin Castle.

"Thank you for the delicious lunch," added Vicki.

"It was my pleasure!" responded the Scarecrow.

The party was lifted into the air once more by the Winged Monkeys. It only took a few minutes to reach the Tin Woodman's Castle.

Once on the ground, the group was able to see some of the statues around the castle of the Tin Woodman's friends including Dorothy, Toto, the Wizard and many, many more. The Tin Man's tin flowers were in bloom. There was a tin pond with live tin fish swimming in it. The castle was made from tin including the towers, minarets, and drawbridge. All of it was bright and glittering.

The Tin Woodman led the way into his castle. He took them into his council chambers. They all sat around a tin table on tin chairs. There were tin vases on the table filled with lovely tin flowers. Tin pictures of the Scarecrow and Tin Woodman decorated the walls.

"Since I have been with you for the last few days," stated the Tin Man, "I don't think I can add anything to what you already know about Ozma's disappearance."

"Have you any magic that might help us find Ozma?" requested Don.

"No. I don't," answered the Tin Woodman. "While I am alive by magic, and I have tin flowers and fish that are alive by magic, I cannot do any magic myself."

"Did you build the castle?" requested Vicki.

"No. The Winkies built it for me. I am their emperor." answered the Tin Man. "Glinda and Ozma provided the magic for the flowers and fish."

"Well, your flowers, fish, and yourself are amazing," remarked Vicki. "You have been a valuable advisor to us."

"You were very helpful in advising us on how to hold court. We couldn't have done it without you," Don assured the Tin Man.

After thanking the Tin Woodman for his hospitality, they all went back outside and got ready to fly to the Old Wicked Witch of the West castle.

It was only a ten minute flight until they landed in the courtyard of the Wicked Witch's castle.

The King offered them light refreshments and gave them a tour of the castle. It included the courtyard where the Cowardly Lion had been imprisoned, and the room where Dorothy was kept. He also told them that the Winged Monkeys were forced to serve the owner of the Golden Cap, which at that time belonged to the Wicked Witch.

"Fortunately, Glinda destroyed the Golden Cap," stated the King. "So now we are free to do as we please."

The group went back to the courtyard. In a few minutes they were airborne once more..

As the passed over the castle, Vicki remarked, "That castle sure looks cold from up here. Of course it was friendly enough while we were inside it."

"It was a very cold place when the Wicked Witch of the West ruled there," assured the Winged Monkey King.

This time they headed for Bear Center. The flight took fifteen minutes.

They landed in a large, circular space in the center of the forest. All the trees surrounding this space were hollow with round holes in their trunks. A little brown bear, with a gun with a tin barrel over his shoulder, stepped out from behind a tree and saluted the group.

"Welcome to Bear Center," greeted the brown bear. "I am Corporal Waddle. What can I do for you?"

"We wish to see your King," responded Glinda.

"One moment please," said the bear, and he raised his gun and pulled the trigger. The tin gun let out a "pop!" as a cork flew out of the barrel. At once bear heads appeared at the holes in each tree.

The Lavender Bear, King of Bear Center came forward to greet his guests. "Welcome!" he called.

"Thank you, Your Majesty for seeing us," said Glinda.

"I am honored to see you again, Vicki and Don," continued the Bear King. "Please, how can I help you?"

"We are honored to see your Bear Center," replied Don.

"If it pleases Your Majesty," added Vicki. "We are seeking magic help in finding Ozma. Do you have any magic that can help us?"

"I do," responded the King Bear. "I can show you what Ozma looks like."

He waved a metal wand three times and Ozma appeared between the King and the travelers.

The Tin Woodman bowed and said, "Your Majesty."

"No!" stated Glinda. "That is not Ozma. It is only an image of her."

"I saw her in my dreams," exclaimed Vicki.

"So did I," added Don.

"Have you other magic?" requested Vicki.

"I have the Little Pink Bear which always speaks the truth," stated the King. "I am willing to use him in your service."

"Could you meet us at the palace in the Emerald City, tomorrow evening?" requested Glinda

"We will be there," the King assured her.

Chapter 11

A Visit to Gillikin Country

As the group got ready to leave Bear Center, the Monkey King asked Glinda, "Where do you want to go next?"

"I think we should drop by Pumperdink," suggested Glinda. "I am sure Vicki and Don will enjoy meeting Kabumpo, among others."

The group was quickly airborne once more.

The first half of the trip was still over yellow fields, homes, and forests.

The last half of the flight was over fields, forests and homes colored purple, for they had entered Gillikin Country which favored the color purple.

As they landed in the courtyard of the palace in Pumperdink, they were met by Prime Pumper.

"What can I do for Your Majesties?" requested the Prime Pumper.

"If you please, we would like to meet with the royal family of Pumperdink," requested Glinda.

"It will be my pleasure to announce your arrival and intentions," stated Prime Pumper.

"ANNOUNCING THE ARRIVAL OF THE TWIN RULERS OF OZ, KING DON AND QUEEN VICKI!" cried the prince. "PLEASE WELCOME . . ."

All who were in Pumperdink could not help but hear the announcement, for Prince Pumper was the chief announcer for all of Pumperdink. He was something like a radio station announcer, but he didn't need a radio.

"Wow! That was quite something," stated Don after his hearing recovered from the announcement.

"Indeed! I don't think we can surprise anyone by our visit now," added Vicki.

After finishing his announcement, Prince Pumper led Don, Vicki, and the others into the Palace. They were quickly invited to join King Pompus the Proud and Queen Pozy Pink in the royal dining room. They were just having a light snack of pastries. Prince Pompadore and his wife Peg Amy, Rulers of Sun Top Mountain were, visiting. Prince Pompadore was the son of the King Pompus and Queen Pozy. Kabumpo an Elegant Elephant was also present. Introductions were made all around.

"This is an honor," remarked King Pompus between bites of a large pastry. "How are things in the Emerald City?"

"Except for the missing people from the palace, all is fine," replied Glinda.

"Please join us for a snack. The cream puffs are delicious!" invited Queen Pozy. "We do have the best pastry cooks in all of Oz."

"Thank you," responded Don. "I don't mind if I do."

They all sat down and had some pastries. Don tried the cream puffs. Vicki had a chocolate éclair. The Hungry Tiger was given a large platter of pastries to himself on the floor at the end of the table. Button-Bright was eating powdered donuts and turning white from all the powdered sugar. The Shaggy Man ate a maple bar. Glinda had a jelly donut or two.

Refreshments were sent out to the courtyard for the Winged Monkeys.

Glinda and the other visitors talked to the royal family about the disappearance of Ozma. When asked if they possessed any magic that might help find Ozma, King Pompus stated that the only magic in Pumperdink was the pastry cooks.

Vicki and Don thanked the royal family for the refreshments.

The royal family of Pumperdink escorted the visitors back to the courtyard. Goodbyes were said and the Winged Monkeys prepared for the next flight.

"Where to from here?" requested the King of the Winged Monkeys.

"I think we should go to the Ruby Palace of Gaylette," responded Glinda. "It is getting late and I think we will make a request to stay there for the night."

"I and my Winged Monkeys are not welcomed there," insisted the King. "Could we instead, put you and the wagon down about a mile from the palace? We would pick you up again in the morning from the same place."

"That should be all right," agreed Glinda.

It took another half hour before they could see the Ruby Palace in the distance. It was an unbelievably beautiful sight as the Red Ruby Palace sparkled at sun set.

The wagon trip took just ten minutes.

Gaylette, the Good Witch of the North, and Quelala greeted the travelers on the steps of the Ruby Palace.

"Welcome to my humble palace!" called Gaylette, as the Tin Woodman, Glinda, Button-Bright, the Shaggy Man, Don, and Vicki undid their seatbelts and got down from the wagon. The Shaggy Man unhitched the Hungry Tiger.

"It is too bad the Winged Monkeys couldn't join us," stated Gaylette.

"Not much escapes your knowledge, does it," stated Glinda. "I believe they didn't think they would be welcome here."

"Not much," agreed Gaylette. "Not after the trick they played on Quelala. Never mind that. Won't you all please come in and have dinner with me? I also have plenty of room to put you up for the night."

A page showed the guests to the quarters for the night. A large feast was waiting for the group in the royal dining room after everyone had freshened up. Once again, Don and Vicki were treated as Rulers of Oz.

Gaylette entertained the guests with what she called some simple acts of magic. Of course Vicki and Don found the acts unbelievable.

After the entertaining was done, Glinda asked, "Gaylette, can you help find Ozma and the other missing people from the palace?"

"I do have a crystal ball," admitted Gaylette. "We could use it to show us Ozma and the others."

"I have always wanted to see a crystal ball," stated Vicki.

"I will have a page get it," replied Gaylette. "Page!"

A page came forward and received directions from Gaylette. The page returned several minutes later with the crystal ball.

Gaylette had the group gather around the ball so that everyone to see what was happening.

"Show us Don and Vicki, Rulers of Oz," commanded Gaylette.

The ball showed the dining room with Vicki and Don in it.

"Now show us Ozma of Oz," requested Gaylette.

The ball showed Ozma's sitting room at the Emerald City Palace. No one was in the room.

"Well, where is Ozma?" asked Don.

"The ball shows her sitting room. That must be where she is," insisted Glinda.

"Crystal ball, please show us Dorothy," said Gaylette.

The ball showed the Wizard's workshop. Once more, it showed no one in the room.

"I don't see Dorothy or anyone else," remarked Vicki.

"Yet the ball insists she is in the workshop at the Emerald City Palace," stated Glinda. "This is strange."

"Gaylette, would you come to a counsel of magic at my palace, tomorrow evening," invited Glinda.

"I don't see how that would do any good," replied Gaylette. "You will only find the answers to your questions at the palace in the Emerald City. However, I will come if that will make you feel better."

"Thank you. It will make me feel better. I appreciate all your assistance," said Glinda. "I don't know about the others, but it has been a long day and I am tired."

"Yes," agreed Vicki.

So did the others.

"I think it is best that we all go to bed," announced Gaylette. "Have a good night sleep."

Gaylette and Quelala rose and left the room. The others went to their quarters. Within minutes, they were all asleep.

Don and Vicki had identical dreams that night. The dreams were about a strange wooden creature with a bent log for a body and head, knotty eyes, and four wooden legs capped with golden feet. There was a mule next to the wooden creature and a small girl.

The next morning, the travelers had breakfast in Glinda's sitting room. A page brought a note stating that Gaylette was tied up all day with business and could they please see themselves off.

During breakfast, Don remarked about a strange dream of a wooden creature with golden capped feet. Somehow, the creature wanted help from Don.

Vicki said she dreamed about that too and it included a mule and a small girl.

"That strange creature sounds like the Wooden Sawhorse of Oz. The mule was Hank the Mule. The small girl was probably Betsy Bobbin," stated Glinda. "They are among those missing from the palace. Somehow those missing from the palace are calling out to you two for help."

"It seems everyone including those who are missing know Don and I are here in Oz to help find the missing," remarked Vicki.

"It figures," stated Don. "Since we are the ones who have to do the work, we are the last to know what it is we are to do."

"Well it should tell you that it is no accident that you two came to the Land of Oz," insisted Glinda. "Somehow you are the key to getting back the missing people."

"I hope we understand what to do soon," said a frustrated Vicki.

Chapter 12

Welcome to Munchkin Country

They continued their trip right after breakfast.

The Winged Monkeys were waiting for them a little ways from the palace. The Hungry Tiger was unhitched and everyone got ready for the trip to Dorothy's old house in Munchkin Country. The wagon was to be returned to the Emerald City.

It took an hour and a half to reach Dorothy's house. During the flight, Don and Vicki got to see more purple forests and fields. About half way through the flight, the fields and forest turned to blue. They had entered Munchkin Country which favored the color blue..

Vicki spotted the Yellow Brick Road just before the group landed next to an old one room house.

Don and Vicki took a look at the old house. They walked around it and peered into the windows.

"So, this is the way Dorothy first came to Oz," remarked Don.

"It was in this house riding a cyclone," stated Vicki. "Of course that was over one-hundred years ago."

"It is amazing that she survived the flight," said Don. "The house should have been destroyed on landing."

"Maybe falling on the Wicked Witch of the East cushioned the fall," suggested Vicki.

"Please don't mention the Wicked Witch of the East," requested a voice from behind them.

They turned around and found a group of small persons standing there. The tallest of these people was about two feet shorter than Vicki.

"Hello, we are Munchkins," stated one of them. "Welcome to Munchkin Country. We were very happy when Dorothy's house landed on the witch. All that was left of the witch were her legs and feet sticking out from under the house."

"Her feet had ruby slippers on them," stated Don.

"Ruby slippers?" questioned one of the Munchkins.

"Oh Don, you must be confused by the movie," interjected Vicki. "It was silver shoes."

"Really?" replied Don.

"Oh yes. It was silver shoes," agreed the Munchkins. "Those shoes were very old and had very powerful magic."

"Too bad Dorothy is missing," replied Don. "The magic of those silver shoes might have been useful."

"Where are the shoes now?" requested Vicki.

"They fell off Dorothy's feet when she used them to return home from her first visit to the Land of Oz," stated a Munchkin. "They land in the Shifting Sand Desert and were destroyed."

"Are you King Don and Queen Vicki, Rulers of Oz?" requested another Munchkin.

"We are," acknowledged Vicki.

"Then you two are great wizards. Surely you can get Dorothy, Ozma, and the others back." stated a third Munchkin.

"They are working on it," Glinda assured the Munchkins.

"Can we see the inside of the house?" requested Vicki.

"I am afraid not," replied one of the Munchkins. "When Dorothy left it, she locked the door. You will have to get the key from her."

"We will do that when we see her," said Don. "It is nice to have met you."

"You are not leaving already are you?" asked the first Munchkin.

"I think we are through here," announced Vicki.

"If it would please Your Majesties, would you kindly come with us and have a snack," requested a fourth Munchkin.

"We mustn't turn down such a kind offer," insisted Don. "We will be happy to come with you. That is, if it is all right with Glinda."

"Of course it is," responded Glinda. "You do want to meet some more of your subjects. These Munchkins are some of the friendliest and fun loving people in Oz."

Don, Vicki, Glinda, Button-Bright, the Shaggy Man, the Tin Man, and the Hungry Tiger followed the Munchkins a few hundred yards to a large picnic area. Here hundreds of Munchkins greeted their new rulers.

There were sweet treats, fruits, vegetables, and many other snacks on the picnic tables. Don and Vicki wanted to be polite and tried a little of everything. They had to give up because they were soon too full to eat another bite. After spending an hour with the Munchkins, it was time to move on.

The Winged Monkeys flew their guests along the Yellow Brick Road for about half an hour. At this point, the Tin Woodman pointed out to his old house in a clearing in the forest below them. Another fifteen minutes of flying and the group could see the Emerald City in the distance. The Winged Monkeys turned south and flew to the Royal College of Oz. Here the party landed between the administration building and a soccer field.

The Professor had his back to the group, as he was watching a soccer game.

"Your students do enjoy their sports," announced Glinda as the group approached the Professor. "May I introduce the Twin Rulers of Oz, Vicki and Don?"

The Professor turned around, bowed and said, "This is an honor. How nice of you busy rulers to take time to visit my humble college."

"Don and Vicki, this is Professor H. M. Wogglebug, T. E. He is the Dean of the Royal College of Oz," stated Glinda.

Vicki got her first good look at the Professor and had to stifle a scream. For she saw that the Professor was a giant bug! He was wearing a top hat and tails, and carried a cane.

Finally, she was able to say, "Oh my!"

The Professor ignored her surprise.

"The H. M. stands for highly magnified," stated Glinda.

"That's for sure," agreed Don, who was also a little uneasy at meeting a six foot tall bug.

"The T. E. stands for Thoroughly Educated," added the proud Professor. "I am sure there is no other wogglebug, but myself, who is so thoroughly educated."

"I can assure you that I have never met another wogglebug as thoroughly educated as you," agreed Vicki. "You are most extraordinary."

"Most wogglebugs are only one-half inches in length," stated Glinda.

"That does make the Professor highly magnified," agreed Don.

"Thank you. Thank you!" replied the Professor. "Perhaps you would like a tour of my college?"

"Yes. That would be great!" agreed Don.

"As you can see, we have many athletic fields for most of the known sports," began the Professor. "And most of my students are hard at work practicing their favorite sports."

"You can see the administration building behind us," continued the Professor.

"The other buildings are classrooms," offered Don.

"Well, the building next to the administration building has rooms for practicing music and other fine arts," agreed the Professor. "The rest of the buildings are dorms for housing the students."

"Where are the classrooms for learning reading, writing, arithmetic, and history?" requested Vicki.

"We don't have classrooms for those subjects," stated the Professor.

"Surely your students need to learn those subjects?" questioned Don.

"Indeed they do," acknowledged the Professor. "If you will follow me to my office, I will show you how my students master those subjects."

The guests followed the Wogglebug into the administration building and down the hall to the Dean's office. They entered the office and saw a large desk. On the wall behind the desk were rows of shelves holding bottles of pills. They bottles had labels on them such as: Grammar, Spelling, Writing, History, Music, Geography, and many, many other subjects.

"My students take two grammar pills each morning," stated the Professor. "For lunch they take math and science pills. Dinner includes writing, spelling, history, and geography pills."

"You mean your students learn these subjects by just taking pills," questioned Don.

"That is exactly what I mean!" stated the Professor.

"Oh that is fabulous!" exclaimed Vicki. "I wish the outside world made learning the easy."

"Here, try one of my geography pills," suggested the Professor, as he took a bottle down from a shelf.

Vicki accepted the pill and took it with a glass of water.

After swallowing the pill, she remarked, "I don't seem to feel any smarter."

"You think not," said the Professor. "Perhaps if I ask you a few questions, you will feel differently."

"How long have you been in the Land of Oz?"

"This is our fourth day here," replied Vicki.

"What surrounds the Land of Oz?"

"Why it is surrounded by a desert," stated Vicki. "No, that isn't entirely true. It is surrounded by four deserts. On the north is the Impassable Desert. On the west is the Deadly Desert. On the south is the Great Sandy Waste. On the east is the Shifting Sands."

"How could you possibly know that?" inquired Don.

"I don't know how I know it," responded Vicki. "I just seem to know it."

"Should we desire to visit the Nome King, we have to go west from Winkie Country," continued Vicki. "You do remember the Nome King, don't you?"

"Yes, I remember the Nome King," said Don. "So, now you know a little about the geography of Oz."

"Oh I know more then just Oz geography," announced Vicki. "For instance, if we want to visit Dunkiton in the Scoodlers, we just go due south from Glinda's Palace."

"Why would we want to go there?" requested Don. "I haven't forgotten that donkey head from their king. On the other hand, we might want to visit Foxville!"

"Foxville! Why would I ever want to go to Foxville? One fox head was enough!" exclaimed Vicki. "Okay. If you insist, you can reach Foxville by going west from Dunkiton."

"Does the geography pill work on outside geography?" asked Don.

"Yes it does," the Professor assured him.

"In the case, Vicki, can you name some of the states we are likely to fly over on our balloon flight?" requested Don.

"Well, we have already gone over California and Arizona," recalled Vicki. "I can give you some of the most probable states we will still have to cross, but the winds could change our course."

"Just give me the next four or five states," said Don.

"Well, we will probably go over New Mexico, then Texas, and Oklahoma. Arkansas is also likely. Then there is either Tennessee or Kentucky, or both," announced Vicki.

"I am impressed," stated Don. "Professor, do you have a pill for music? Specifically, do you have a pill to help me play a trumpet better?"

"I do have a pill that will teach you about music, how to read it, and the theory of playing a trumpet," responded the Professor. "However, playing the trumpet is a mechanical skill, which is much more than just a mental skill. Mechanical skills cannot be learned from a pill. You have to practice and practice, just like you would for any sport."

"He needs all the help he can get," remarked Vicki. "Please give him a music pill."

The Professor got Don a music pill, which Don took. However, Don declined to demonstrate his ability with a trumpet.

"Professor, do you have any magic pills that might help us find Ozma," requested Glinda.

"While the pills I give to my students to help them learn mental skills are magical, I myself do not have any other magic," replied the Professor.

"Thank you, Professor, for a look at your college," announced Glinda. "We have taken up enough of your time."

"It is always a pleasure to have company," insisted the Professor.

"I think it is time for us to journey to my castle," stated Glinda. "Goodbye Professor."

Everyone else said their goodbyes.

Chapter 13

Sight Seeing in Quadling Country

Just before the group was airborne again, Glinda requested, "King of the Winged Monkeys, could we please stop by China Country. Just set us down outside the gate to their country."

"It would be our pleasure," said the Winged Monkey King, as he bowed to Glinda.

The travelers were quickly on their way. For the first few moments they flew over blue fields, forests, and houses. As they crossed into Quadling Country the houses, forest, and fields changed to red as the favorite color.

An hour later the monkeys landed the visitors at the entrance to China Country.

There was a sign next to the gate to China Country. It read:

WELCOME TO CHINA COUNTRY
We are brittle and break easily, so
PLEASE, just go away!

Don remarked, "That is an unusual thing to say. What is wrong with these people?"

"There is nothing wrong with them," stated Vicki. "Don't you remember meeting the Princess of China Country at our court session? These people are all live china figurines."

"That's right. The princess was only a foot tall," recalled Don. "Come on. Let's visit the princess!"

"If you folks don't mind, I think I will wait for you out here," requested the Hungry Tiger. "One accidental swish of my tail could damage many of the china citizens."

"It doesn't look like they really want visitors," said Vicki.

"Don't let the sign bother you," insisted Glinda. "They will be trilled to meet the new Rulers of Oz. Come on."

Glinda led the way to the gate and rang a bell next to it.

A few moments passed and then a small china man stuck his head through a small window at the bottom of the gate.

"Can't you read the sign? Please just go away," called the man as he looked up at the visitors.

"We wish to see your Princess," stated Glinda. "Tell her the new Twin Rulers of Oz are here to visit her."

"By all means Your Majesties," replied the startled man. "One moment, please. I will convey your request to our Princess."

Several minutes later, the gate was opened by the small china man. Trumpets sounded, and a herald announced, "The Princess of China Country."

"Welcome to China Country. Please keep a safe distance from all our inhabitants," requested the Princess.

Don started to walk up to the Princess. He saw the frightened look on her face and halted. The Princess relaxed.

"It is best to leave a yard or two between us and the inhabitants of this land," cautioned Glinda. "Stay on the gravel path. Make no sudden moves."

"Please, won't you join us for tea," requested the Princess.

"We would be delighted!" answered Vicki. "You and your land are so beautiful."

As the group walked slowly down the path toward the Princess's palace, they saw many fine china homes, a school, a church, and stores. There were china boys and girls playing in china streets. There were china cattle and sheep in the fields eating china grass. China pigs were in the barnyards. A china milkmaid was milking a china cow.

A table was set up outside the palace for the big visitors to sit at. Tea and cakes were served. Don had several cakes. Vicki enjoyed the tea. There was talk about how to find Ozma and what magic was available from

China Country. Unfortunately, the only magic in China Country was the ability of the china figurines to be alive.

The group walked slowly back to the country gate.

The Princess said goodbye to the visitors.

Shortly thereafter, the group was lifted into the sky and continued on their way to Glinda's Palace. The flight took an hour.

Part of Glinda's all girl army greeted the travelers. The army wore red uniforms trimmed with real gold braid.

Don couldn't take his eyes off of the girl soldiers.

"Men!" remarked a disappointed Vicki.

"Don't be too hard on him," cautioned Glinda. "My army is chosen for their beauty, charm, and intelligence. Don, will get over it in a couple of minutes."

"Come everyone," directed one of the soldiers. "I will show you to your quarters."

Everyone followed the girl soldier to their quarters.

They were able to rest up before dinner. Changes of clothes were provided for them all, which is just as well, as Glinda announce they would be attending a formal dinner.

Much to Don's delight, two girl soldiers a piece were appointed for escorts to each guest. The girl soldiers, or rather the lady soldiers were wearing their formal uniforms. They looked even more beautiful than before.

All the others persons who had been invited to the Council of Magic were also at the formal dinner,

Glinda entertained them as royal guests. The food, as usual, was great!

Although Vicki did not consider Don to be a boy friend, she was jealous of all the attention Don paid to the girl soldiers. After all, when Cousin Don was with her, he usually paid most of his attention to her.

As the meal progressed, Vicki relaxed a little and got to talking with her escort of lady soldiers. At first the talk was about fashions and music trends in the outside world. The longer they talked, the more Vicki got interested in her escorts. They were not only beautiful, but very knowledgeable and friendly. And their manners were impeccable.

Vicki asked one of the soldiers if she was in the same army that had greeted Dorothy when she was on her first visit to the Land of Oz.

The soldier replied that she was one of the girl soldiers who had greeted Dorothy when Dorothy first visited Glinda's castle.

"But that was over one-hundred years ago!" remarked Vicki.

"Indeed it was," agreed the soldier.

"Why that would make you at least one-hundred and twenty-five years old!" exclaimed Vicki.

"Oh, I am a little older than that, my dear," responded the soldier. "All the natives of the Land of Oz are. Why, unless we want to, none of us have aged a day since the Fairy Queen Lurline made the Land of Oz centuries ago."

All Vicki could think of to say was, "Wow!"

"While you are in the Land of Oz, you don't age either," explained soldier on the other side of Vicki. "Take Button Bright; how old do you think he is?"

"Why Button Bright looks like a six year old," responded Vicki.

"He was six years old when he moved to the Land of Oz," agreed the soldier. "That was about one-hundred and five years ago!"

"Oh my," said Vicki. "That would make him around one-hundred and ten years old."

"Yes it would," agreed the soldier.

Vicki continued to talk with her escorts during the whole meal. She had forgotten all about being mad at Don for his giving all his attention to the girl soldiers.

As the meal finished, Vicki was able to take Don aside.

"Don, what did you think of you dinner companions?" asked Vicki.

"They were very charming," replied Don. "They were also very knowledgeable."

"Yes they are very charming," agreed Vicki. "How old do you think they are?".

"Why I would guess they are a little older then me," answered Don.

"Perhaps they are older than you think," added Vicki.

"Oh!" remarked Don. "How much older than me do you think the girl soldier on my right was?"

"She is hundreds of years older than you," stated Vicki with a snicker. "I guess you could say you have fallen for an older woman."

"Oh me, oh my!" remarked a disbelieving Don.

Chapter 14

A Magic Council is Held

After dinner, Gaylette, Glinda, the Tin Woodman, the Scarecrow, the Hungry Tiger, the Shaggy Man, Button Bright, Don, and Vicki were gathered together in Glinda's quarters in Glinda's castle, in Quadling Country. They were watching Glinda read from the Great Book of Records.

"Vicki and Don, you were made Joint Rulers of Oz because the Great Book of Records said you should be the next Rulers of Oz," announced Glinda. "It wasn't because of any thunderstorm or other freak accident. Your to become Rulers of Oz was in the next entry after the notice that a magical accident had occurred in the Emerald City, causing the disappearance of Ozma."

"The magical accident was what?" asked Vicki

"That would be all the persons in the palace disappearing and June 20 repeating over and over," stated Gaylette.

"The Book of Records told all of that. Amazing!" added Don.

"The book's entries are not that complete," admitted Glinda. "A messenger from the Emerald City told me about the missing people. Our unchanging calendars told about the date problem."

"But the book did tell you that Don and I were coming to Oz, didn't it?" requested Vicki.

"Not exactly," replied Glinda. "It does show everything that is going on in the world that affects the Land of Oz. Your trying for the ballooning record was listed. So I knew you had some connection with the Land of Oz."

"Okay, you knew ahead of time that Don and I were coming to Oz to be your new rulers," stated Vicki. "Why must it be us? We are nothing special."

"Surely some local citizens of Oz could rule you better than us," insisted Don.

"For some reason, Oz needs you two," stated Gaylette. "I don't know why, but you two have some special powers."

"No, we don't!" said Don and Vicki in unison. "We are not special."

"Do that again," requested Glinda.

"Do what?" asked Vicki and Don together.

"You both said the same thing at the same time," announced the Tin Woodman. "You can do twin talk!"

"Big deal!" responded Don and Vicki.

"Don. You do the talking," requested Vicki. "Twin talking is tiresome."

"Okay. Vicki and I can twin talk for short periods of time," agreed Don. "What is so great about that? Any two people can learn to do that."

"You are wrong," insisted Glinda. "Not just any two people can do twin talk. Just because you two can do twin talk doesn't make it easy."

"You were made joint or Twin Rulers of the Land of Oz for some purpose," said Gaylette. "Exactly why you were made rulers will become more evident as we find the cause and solution to our mystery. But don't knock twin talk. Not many people can do it."

"Okay. We agree that we are special," said Vicki and Don together. "We just didn't think a simple trick like twin talk could be considered to be magical."

"You are Twin Rulers of Oz, that can do twin talk," stated the Tin Woodman. "That makes you doubly special."

"If Gaylette and Glinda think you two are special, believe them," warned the Shaggy Man. "The Land of Oz does need you."

Button Bright added, "Needed. Special!"

"Okay. Okay. We are special," agreed Don and Vicki. "How is that going to help the Land of Oz? Do you really think twin talk will have anything to do with it?"

"That is yet to be determined," added Gaylette. "Be patient. I am sure all will be made clear to you in a little while. The more I am around you two the more I think Glinda is right. You two are special and the Land of Oz needs you right now! However, I think you need to be in the Emerald City Palace to find out the answers. That is where the problem started and that is where the solution must be found."

"I think Gaylette is right. We must now return to the Emerald City," announced Glinda. "There is nothing more that we can do here to solve this mystery."

"I think I will return home," stated Gaylette. "I know you can solve this problem once you get back to the Emerald City. Good Luck."

The Hungry Tiger, the Tin Woodman, Button-Bright, the Shaggy Man, Glinda, Don, and Vicki walked out into the palace courtyard.

"Winged Monkey King, I have one last request for you," said Glinda.

"What might that be?" requested the King.

"Please take all of us back to the palace in the Emerald City," requested Glinda. "That will be the end of our trip. Thank you for your help."

"Have you found Ozma?" asked the King.

"No, but we expect to shortly," Glinda assured him. "Have no fear. Please just take us to the Emerald City."

"My monkeys are at your command. Please get in your swings," responded the Monkey King. "It is almost dark. We want to hurry. If possible, we wish to be done flying by dark."

"That would be fine with us," agreed Don and Vicki. "Please allow us to put you up at the palace for the night."

"We would be most honored to stay at the palace," replied the King of the Monkeys with a bow.

The group got into their swings. The flight headed for the Emerald City.

The trip to the Emerald City took just an hour. It was evening by the time they got there. The green Emerald City sparkled in the night sky. The balloon could be seen out in the field lit up by magic spotlights.

Seeing the balloon made Vicki and Don homesick. Would they ever get to finish their balloon trip? How were their families taking the missing balloonist? The two of them had almost forgotten about their families.

Once they reached the palace, the group went to Ozma's sitting room in Ozma's quarters.

Chapter 15

The Magic Mirror is consulted

Glinda, the Tin Woodman, the Shaggy Man, Button Bright, the Hungry Tiger, Vicki, and Don gathered in Ozma's sitting room. They appeared to be the only ones in the sitting room. There was no sign of Ozma.

Glinda showed Don and Vicki a picture hanging on the wall. It looked like a peaceful country scene. It certainly didn't seem to be anything special.

"What a nice peaceful scene," remarked Vicki. She was puzzled by why Glinda has pointed it out.

"This is the Magic Picture," announced Glinda. "It is a national treasure of Oz."

"Sort of like a Picasso or Monet painting," suggested Don. "So, it is worth millions of dollars."

"Well, it is priceless," agreed Glinda, "but not because it is great art. Let me demonstrate it to you."

"Magic Picture, please show us where Don and Vicki, Joint Rulers of Oz, are right now," requested Glinda.

The picture changed to show the sitting room with the Tin Woodman, Vicki, Don, and Glinda in it.

"That is great!" exclaimed Vicki. "Now it is a mirror."

"Actually it is a little more useful than a mirror," remarked Glinda. "It can show us anyone anywhere in the world."

"It can show us anyone?" questioned Don. "Wherever they are in the world?"

"Yes, anyone anywhere in the world," repeated Glinda. "Let's try something else. Magic Picture, show us Vicki's mother."

The picture changed to show Vicki's mother watching news broadcasts about the balloon flight. She looked very worried.

"Oh my, Auntie Peggy seems worried," stated Don. "She is just waiting at home for the results of our balloon flight. That is nerve racking. I wonder if she has heard about the thunderstorm."

"I hope we can solve this problem quickly so we can get back to our balloon flight," remarked Vicki. "I don't like to see Mother worrying like this."

"Yes. It is time to work some more on our mystery," agreed Glinda. "Magic Picture, show us Ozma!"

The picture changed back to show the sitting room with the Tin Woodman, Vicki, Don, and Glinda in it.

"That doesn't make sense. It is just showing us again," announced Vicki to no one in particular.

"So, why isn't it showing us Ozma?" requested Don. "You did say it could show us anyone anywhere in the world."

"Yes I did," stated Glinda. "And it does. If I knew the answer to that question, our mystery would be solved! All I can tell you is that the Magic Picture has always shown what we requested. Therefore Ozma must be here in this room even if we can't see her. And if she is here, then for some reason she isn't able to contact us. This is very strange!"

"Perhaps we will have better luck with someone else that is missing?" suggested Vicki."Can anyone command the picture?"

"Yes. Why don't you give it try?" responded Glinda.

"Okay. Show us Billina and her chicks?" requested Vicki.

The Picture changed to show a far corner of the throne room. Once again it didn't show the requested being.

"I do remember smelling chickens in that corner of the throne room," recalled Vicki. "But I couldn't find any trace of the chickens entering or leaving the throne room. Now the Magic Picture thinks there are chickens there as well."

"May I try it?" requested Don.

"By all means," agreed Glinda.

"Magic Picture, show Dorothy, Toto, and the Wizard," commanded Don

The Picture changed to show the Wizard's laboratory. Specifically, it showed the workbench area in the laboratory. Toto, Dorothy, and the Wizard were not visible.

"Can we see the Cowardly Lion?" asked Vicki.

The Picture showed a corner of the stable.

"Well there was a strange smell in the stables that King Kik-a-Bray said was the smell of a large lion," remembered Don. "The smell was very strong like the lion was still there."

"Please show us the Wooden Sawhorse of Oz," said Glinda.

The Picture changed to the right, but was still showing part of the stables.

"Show us Hunk the Mule and Betsy Bobbin," requested Vicki.

The picture showed another part of the stables.

"I remember smelling a mule there," remarked Don. "However, I don't see how this is getting us anywhere closer to solving the mystery."

"Sure we are," replied Glinda. "Every time we ask to see one of the creatures or people that disappeared, the Magic Picture always shows us part of the palace."

"The Picture is working correctly, isn't it?" inquired Vicki.

"Oh it is working just fine!" stated Glinda. "For instance, Magic Picture, please show us the Scarecrow of Oz."

The Picture changed to show the Scarecrow in his study in his Ear of Corn shaped house.

"Okay," agreed Don. "The Magic Picture is working just fine."

"In that case, we just need to figure out what the Picture is trying to tell us," summarized Vicki. "Then the whole mystery will be solved."

Is the Magic Picture working correctly?

Will the Magic Picture be believed?

Chapter 16

The Little Pink Bear is consulted

Glinda, the Shaggy Man, Button Bright, the Hungry Tiger, Vicki, Don, and Tin Woodman were still sitting in Ozma's sitting room trying to figure out what the Magic Picture had shown them, when a page announced, "His Majesty, the Big Lavender Bear, King of Bear Center in Winkie Country, and the Bear Center National Treasure, the Little Pink Bear."

The Big Lavender Bear entered Ozma's sitting room carrying the Little Pink Bear.

The bear bowed to Vicki and Don, and said, "Your Majesties, I wish to offer the help of our national treasure of Bear Center, the Little Pink Bear, in helping you solve the mystery of Ozma's disappearance,"

"Welcome, Your Majesty and Bear Center National Treasure. Thank you for coming," responded Glinda. "We are delighted to see you."

"How can you help us?" requested Don.

"Why this Little Pink Bear can answer any question you ask it," stated the Lavender Bear. "His answers are always correct!"

"But he looks like a stuffed teddy bear," remarked Vicki. "He doesn't seem to move at all!"

"Nevertheless, when I turn this crank in his side, he will answer your question," insisted the Lavender Bear.

"However, I must warn you to be respectful to the Little Pink Bear," stated a very serious Bear. "The last time I had the Pink Bear tell where to find Ozma, no one believed him. It was most upsetting to him."

"We will be most grateful for any help the Pink Bear offers to us," Glinda assured the Lavender Bear. "It is easy for people to misunderstand advice. Thank you for coming and offering to help."

"I am only too happy to help the Rulers of Oz," responded the bear with a bow.

"May we find the wisdom to understand the Pink Bear's wise answers," said Vicki. "We are new at taking magical advice. Please be patient with us."

"Respect the Pink Bear and all will be well," answered the Lavender Bear. "You just have to believe what he says is always correct!"

"Vicki, perhaps you have a question for the bear," suggested Don. "Go ahead and ask it."

"Okay," agreed Vicki. "Where is Ozma?"

The room became very still.

The Big Lavender Bear turned the crank of the Little Pink Bear.

Then they heard the Pink Bear said, "Ozma is in our presence!"

Everyone looked around the sitting room. Ozma was no where to be seen or heard.

"Are you sure the bear understood the question?" asked a puzzled Don.

"Yes," replied the Big Bear. "Perhaps you would prefer to ask a question?"

"What room is Ozma in?" questioned Don.

The Lavender Bear turn the crank in the side of the Little Pink Bear one more time.

"Ozma is in her sitting room," replied the Little Bear.

"Well that is clear enough," stated Glinda. "Ozma is here in this room. Perhaps she has been transformed so we don't recognize her."

"Has Ozma been transformed to another shape?" requested Glinda of the Little Pink Bear.

The crank was turned. The Little Bear said, "No!"

"Okay, Ozma is here in this room. She has not been transformed into another shape. So, why can't we see and hear her?" requested Vicki.

"Are you asking the Little Pink Bear that question?" responded the Big Bear.

"Yes!" replied Vicki. "I believe I am. Wise Pink Bear, why can't we see and hear Ozma?"

Once more, the crank was turned on the Little Bear.

"Because Ozma cannot see or hear you," stated the Little Pink Bear.

"Let's try another question," suggested Glinda. "Where is the Wizard of Oz?"

The Big Bear turned the crank.

"The Wizard is in his workshop," replied the Little Pink Bear.

"Where are Dorothy and Toto?" asked Don.

The Lavender Bear turn the crank once more.

"They are with the Wizard," responded the Pink Bear.

"That seems straight forward enough," announced Glinda. "The bear is saying the Ozma and the Wizard never left the palace. Thank you, Little Pink Bear and Big Lavender Bear."

"I am always glad to help the Rulers of Oz," said the Big Lavender Bear, as he bowed to Vicki, Don and Glinda.

"Yes. Thank you!" echoed Don and Vicki together. "We will let you know if we have any more questions."

"Just remember this," stated the Lavender bear. "The Little Pink Bear never makes a mistake. His answers are to be respected, not insulted."

Finally, the Big Bear said, "Just because one does not understand the answers doesn't make them untrue."

The Big Bear bowed once more and left the room carrying the Little Pink Bear.

"When you request answers from a magical object, the answers may not be all that clear," advised Glinda. "However, the Big Lavender Bear's advice is good. You can trust the answers given to you by the Little Pink Bear."

"Those answers seem to agree with what the Magic Picture showed us," stated a confused Vicki.

"Now, if we can just find the wisdom to understand all the answers we have received," added a bewildered Don.

"It begins to look more and more like Gaylette was right," admitted Glinda. "The answers to the mystery must be somewhere here in the palace."

Will the new Rulers of Oz have the wisdom to understand the answers given by the crystal ball, the Magic Mirror, the Little Pink Bear, and their noses when they had a fox and donkey head?

Chapter 17

Glinda Explains the Picture and Bear's Answers

"Let me summarize what we have been told," said Glinda. "The Magic Picture showed us this sitting room when we asked where is Ozma."

"True," agreed Don. "However, we can't seem to see or hear her here."

"We asked to see Billina and her chicks, and the picture showed us the far corner of the throne room," added Vicki. "That is where King Dox and I smelled live chickens."

"The Picture showed the Wizard's laboratory when we asked to see Dorothy, Toto, and the Wizard," recalled Glinda.

"The stable was shown when we ask to see Cowardly Lion and the Wooden Sawhorse of Oz," stated Don. "Of course we didn't see them either."

"King Kik-a-Bray did smell a large lion in the stables," insisted Vicki. "However we didn't find the lion. I thought that was strange at the time. He and Don also smelled the mule."

"Okay. We are remembering the same things," agreed Glinda. "You should know that the Magic Picture has never been wrong."

"Now, you sound like the Big Lavender Bear," remarked Don. "He said the Little Pink Bear always tells the truth."

"That means Ozma is here in this sitting room, right now!" said Glinda. "For both the Bear and the Picture agree to that."

"So did Gaylette's crystal ball," added the Tin Woodman. "Everything points to Ozma being in this room."

"Of course, she is here but we can't see or hear her," repeated Vicki. "How are we to find and help her? This is very confusing."

"Does Ozma know any magic that could cause people to disappear or the day to repeat?" asked Don.

"She doesn't do that type of magic," insisted Glinda. "Outside of using the Magic Belt, her magic is done with a magic wand."

"Do you see her wand anywhere?" requested Vicki. "Is there any sign that she was doing magic?"

Everyone looked around for a magic wand and other signs that Ozma might have been doing some type of magic. Nothing was found.

"Perhaps we need to look for someone else first," suggested Don. "Maybe then we can find a clue to Ozma's disappearance."

"Like whom?" requested Vicki.

Don suggested, "How about the Wizard? The Great Book of Records said some type of magical accident took place. The Wizard does know some magic, doesn't he?"

"Yes. I have taught the Wizard many magic tricks and spells," Glinda informed them. "I know the Wizard has also worked on learning some other spells without my help."

"Do you know any magic that would account for the missing people and stuck calendar?" requested Don.

"No! I don't," answered Glinda.

"Does the Wizard know any spells like that?" asked Vicki.

"Not that I know of," responded Glinda. "Of course he might have learned them on his own."

"Could it be the Wizard was trying to do a new spell and had an accident?" suggested Don. "You said he isn't as good with magic as you are."

"A magical accident caused by the Wizard," mused Glinda. "That is a possibility."

"I believe you are on the right track, cousin," agreed Vicki. "Let's stop worrying about Ozma for now and see if we can find the Wizard of Oz."

"In that case, we need to go to the Wizard's Laboratory," announced Glinda "That is where the Magic Picture, the crystal ball, and the Little Pink Bear say the Wizard is. Come on, I will lead the way."

I smell the Wizard, Dorothy, Toto, and someone else.

Chapter 18

The Source of the Spell Uncovered

Glinda, the Hungry Tiger, the Shaggy Man, Button Bright, and the Tin Woodman accompanied Don and Vicki to the Wizard's Laboratory or Workshop. They stopped at the Workshop door. The door, which had a doggie door in it, was locked. They knocked on the door but no one answered their knock.

"Glinda, do you have a key to the Workshop?" requested Vicki.

"No. But don't worry about it," responded Glinda.

Glinda took out her magic wand and said a few magic words. The lock clicked and the door opened.

"Why couldn't you just do that to front door of the palace?" requested Don. "That way you could have gotten in here two and a half weeks ago."

"Because the palace is protected on the outside by an anti-spell, spell," explained Glinda. "I thought everyone knew that."

"Tin Woodman, you knew that, didn't you?" requested Vicki.

"Yes, I did," agreed the Tin Man.

"So, Don and I couldn't have used magic to get into the palace, after all," summarized Vicki.

"That is true, but I was hoping you might have special powers for opening the door," admitted the Tin Woodman. "After all, you two had been made the new Rulers of Oz."

"We did have special powers," stated Don. "They were called an anchor and rope."

"Hungry Tiger, would you please see what smells you can find here in the Workshop," requested Glinda. "The Wizard, Dorothy, and Toto are supposed to be in here somewhere."

The Tiger entered the Workshop and walked around the room, sniffing as he went. He found the area near the workbench interesting. After several minutes of sniffing around the workbench, he stopped and faced the other.

"This is strange," stated the confused Tiger. "It smells like the Wizard is standing in front of the workbench, with Dorothy and Toto on his left. And, there is someone else."

"But there is no one there at all!" said Don. "That is strange."

"That is no stranger than my smelling Billina and her chicks in the throne room," recalled Vicki. "Wasn't your smelling the mule and lion just as strange?"

"Okay, you win," replied Don. "As strange as it may seem, the Wizard, Dorothy, and Toto must be in this room!"

Don, Vicki, Glinda, and the Tin Woodman walked over to the workbench.

They found the Wizards notebook lying opened next to an old magic spell book. The spell book was also open.

Glinda looked at the spell book.

"This is interesting," remarked Glinda."The book is open to a spell used to make people disappear temporarily."

"How temporarily?" asked Don.

"I don't know," replied Glinda

"Where do they disappear to?" inquired Vicki.

"I don't know," answered Glinda.

"If they just disappear temporarily, how do we get them back?" asked the Tin Woodman.

"I suppose that is accomplished by some counter spell," stated Glinda. "Let me read the spell and counter spell. But first let me look at this other spell that is book marked."

Glinda put another book mark in the page for making people disappear. She closed the book

"Here is another thing to add to our list of strange things," announced Glinda. "This is one of old Mombi the Witch's old spell book. It should have been destroyed. Its title is: Book of Twin Spells!"

"Did you say twin spells?" requested Don.

"Yes, I did," responded Glinda.

"Does that have anything to do with us being twin rulers?" asked Vicki.

"It might, or it might not! Let's look at the other marked spell," suggested Glinda. She opened the book to the other book mark.

Glinda read over the spell. "This spell is used for making a day repeat in time."

"It sounds like we might have found the source of the spells affecting Oz," said Don. "Now what do we do?"

"At least we know the answer to the mystery of the disappearing people and the locked up calendar," stated Vicki. "That is a big step forward toward solving our problems."

"That is fine!" agreed Don. "We know the cause. Now we need to find the cure."

"Let me read over both spells and their counter spells," requested Glinda. "This may take a few minutes. Please be patient. After I finish reading them we can decide what to do next."

Glinda sat reading the spell books for fifteen minutes. Vicki and Don were afraid to interrupt her. She even looked over some of the other spells in the book. Finally, Glinda looked up from the book.

"All the spells in this book require two persons to say the spell together," remarked Glinda. "That is why it is called the Book of Twin Spells."

A confused Vicki remarked, "How nice!"

"However," continued Glinda. "The counter spell to making people disappear is more complicated. It requires that the counter spell be said by the Twin Rulers of Oz."

"Have there been other Twin Rulers of Oz?" asked Don.

"No, there haven't been any Twin Rulers of Oz before," stated Glinda.

"It sounds like Mombi the Witch meant for the people she made disappear to remain disappeared," remarked Vicki. "She didn't expect there to ever be any Twin Rulers of Oz!"

"So it would seem," agreed Don.

Glinda announced, "You two were right! Your being Twin Rulers of Oz does have something to do with the counter spell for the disappearing people. So now we know why you two had to come to the Land of Oz and be made the Rulers of Oz."

"Fine!" replied Vicki and Don, together. "After that counter spell is done, then we can return to our balloon flight."

"I believe so," acknowledged Glinda. "The repeating calendar day spell seems to be independent of the disappearing people spell."

"What are we waiting for?" requested Vicki. "Let's say the counter spell and get on our way in our balloon."

"Let us not be too haste," warned Glinda. "There has already been one magical accident associated with the disappearing spell. We don't need to rush into making another magical accident."

"Okay," agreed Don and Vicki together. "We can spare a little more time for working on this problem. We do want to do everything correctly!"

"Good!" stated Glinda. "That is a very sensible attitude to take when working with magic. Never be in a rush when working with magic! There is no telling what can happen if you do a spell wrong!"

Will Don and Vicki get to say the spell?

Will they say it right?"

If not, what will happen?"

Chapter 19

Ozma and the Others Are Released From Spell

"What do we do to get Ozma and the others released from the disappearing spell?" asked Don.

"The spell book has a counter spell or reappearing spell," announced Glinda. "It has some special conditions for using it."

"I can guess," said Vicki. "We have to say the first part of it standing on our left feet, the next part standing on our right feet, and the last part with our eyes closed."

"No, it is more like you have to hug each other very tightly, and kiss each other after every third word," stated Glinda with a smile.

"Oh yuck!" remarked Vicki. "You can't be serious."

"She could be serious," insisted Don. "After all we had to get tossed into the Truth Pond to restore our normal heads! Relax! Maybe Glinda will furnish us with some mistletoe."

"That would make it easier," agreed Vicki. "I just wish we had known all the things we had to do before we accepted these crowns."

"Look! I was kidding," said Glinda. "There is no kissing or hugging. However, the counter spell can only be said by Twin Rulers of Oz."

"You are kidding again, aren't you?" said Vicki.

"No, I am not," insisted Glinda. "See this note at the bottom of the spell. It says it must be said by the Twin Rulers of Oz."

"How soon will we be doing the spell?" asked Don.

"The sooner the better, I think. I will try to make it easy for you," Glinda assured them. "I believe the first step is to have each of you read over this counter spell page."

Vicki read over the page shown to her by Glinda. When she was finished, Don read the page.

"Good. This doesn't say anything about hugging and kissing during the spell!" insisted Don.

"It just says that twin rulers have to use twin talk as they say the spell," added a confused Vicki.

"Okay. Okay!" said Glinda, "I said I was joking about the hugs and kisses. However, it is important that you say every thing is unison. Do you two think you can do that?"

"What? You want us to say the same thing at the same time?" requested Don and Vicki in unison. "Isn't that part of why we are called the Twin Rulers of Oz?"

"Possibly," agreed Glinda. "That is what you need to do to make this counter spell work. But be warned! If it isn't done exactly in unison, bad things might happen."

Don inquired, "What kind of bad things?"

"I am not sure," replied Glinda. "My best guess is that you two will also disappear!"

"Then we better get it right," stated Vicki. "Don, I think we better read over the spell again."

"Good idea!" agreed Don. "Let's make sure we can pronounce all the words correctly."

Glinda helped Don and Vicki practice saying each of the difficult words. This wasn't easy because not just anyone can pronounce words like pfzxqw and kjsvwt.

Finally Vicki and Don were ready to try and do the spell.

They got in sync by counting out loud the words one, two, three, and then recited the spell, word for word, perfectly.

All a sudden, Don was knocked over by the reappearing Wizard. Dorothy knocked over Vicki. Glinda was just able to avoid stepping on Toto as he appeared at her feet. A page appeared off to their right.

"Oh wow!" exclaimed Vicki. "I never knew I could do magic. That was kind of exciting!"

"The Tin Woodman did say we were a great Witch and a great Sorcerer," Don reminded Vicki. "But, I still don't believe we actually made a spell work."

"What happened?" cried the startled page. "I seem to remember being here and not being here. Now, I am here again."

"You disappeared for two and one half weeks," replied Don.

"Oh dear!" exclaimed the page.

"Don't worry," Vicki assured the page, "There is nothing to worry about. You are fine now."

"That is easy for you to say. My mother will be worried sick," called the excited page as he ran from the room.

"Who are you? What are you doing in my workshop?" requested the Wizard as he saw Don and Vicki for the first time.

"They just restored you to this world," stated Glinda. "You should be grateful to the new Rulers of Oz."

The Wizard turned and took a better look at Don and Vicki. He said, "Thank you, Your Majesties."

Dorothy added her thanks. Toto even barked his thanks.

"Did you say the new Rulers of Oz?" asked the confused Wizard. "Are they both ruling Oz?"

"It is a long story. We can get to it in a little while," responded Glinda.

"Shouldn't we see if Ozma is back?" suggested Vicki. "That is why we were doing the spell, wasn't it?"

"That is a good idea," agreed Glinda. "Let's all go the Ozma's quarters and see if she is back."

Glinda led the way with the others right behind her. A few minutes later, they reached Ozma's quarters.

Glinda knocked on the door. A voice responded with, "Come in."

Everyone entered the sitting room of Ozma.

Ozma looked at the two strangers. "Who are these people?" she requested.

"Ozma, may I introduce the new Joint Rulers of Oz, Vicki and Don," answered Glinda.

"Did you say the new Rulers of Oz?" questioned Ozma. "I thought I was the Ruler of All of Oz."

"You were until two and a half week ago," stated the Tin Woodman. "Then you disappeared."

"Three days ago, Don and Vicki were crowded Rulers of All Oz," stated Glinda. "Without their help, we would not have been able to unlock the palace and would never have found you."

"Where have I been?" requested a confused Ozma.

"As near as we can tell, you have been right here in your sitting room," replied the Tin Woodman. "However, no one could see or hear you."

"You said the palace was locked up?" questioned Ozma. "I don't understand. We never lock the palace."

"I have been locking the palace at around midnight each night," stated the Wizard. "It just seemed like a good idea. Besides, if anyone needs to get in the palace later at night, they can ring the door bell."

"My palace has a door bell?" questioned Ozma.

"It does now," said the Wizard.

"I think we should stop locking up the palace unless we are expecting trouble," stated Ozma. "We are not expecting trouble, are we?"

"No," admitted the Wizard.

"So, when did I disappear? What day is today?" requested Ozma.

"You disappeared on June 20," stated Don.

"Today is still June 20," added Vicki.

"Let me get this straight. I disappeared on June 20, which was two and a half weeks ago," said Ozma. "And now, two and a half weeks later it is still June 20."

"That is about the size of it," admitted the Wizard.

"It has been June 20, for two and a half weeks," explained the Tin Man.

"I find this difficult to believe!" announced Ozma. "Has some magic been used on me?"

"Yes, some magic was used on you," responded Glinda.

"Wizard, do you know something about this magic?" asked Ozma.

"Yes Your Majesty," answered the Wizard. "I think I can explain what happened."

"Please do!" commanded Ozma.

"Well, Your Majesty, it all started with you saying what a great time you had on June 20, and how you wished you could do it again," continued the Wizard

"I see! So now you are going to blame this on me. Please continue," remarked Ozma.

"Well, Dorothy and I were looking around the treasury and came upon an old magic book of Mombi the Witch," continued the Wizard. "It was called the Twin Book of Magic."

"The twin part referred to the requirement of two people saying a spelling to make it work," volunteered Dorothy.

"Anyway, we found a spell for making a calendar day repeat," stated the Wizard.

"The Wizard and I said the spell and it has been June 20 ever since," finished Dorothy.

"Can you undo this spell?" requested Ozma.

"Yes Your Majesty," the Wizard assured her. "We just have to do the counter spell."

"Good! We can take care of that later," said Ozma. "However, that doesn't explain why I disappeared for two and a half weeks."

"It wasn't just you, Ozma," said Don.

"It was everyone in the palace," added Vicki.

"Oh my!" remarked Ozma. "Did that include the Wizard and Dorothy?"

"Yes it did," announced Glinda. "It included the Cowardly Lion, Billina and her chicks, The Wooden Sawhorse, Hank the Mule, Betsy Bobbin, and everyone else in the palace. It happened late at night, so the palace was locked up."

"So, how long did it take to find out I was missing?" requested Ozma.

"Well, we knew something was wrong the next day," stated the Tin Woodman.

"Of course the Great Book of Records reported the magical accident," added Glinda. "It also mentioned that two outsiders would soon be the new Twin Rulers of Oz."

"How did I happen to disappear?" asked Ozma.

"Well, Dorothy and I were reciting the spell to make a person disappear temporarily," said the Wizard. "We had one of the pages volunteer."

"We had just reached the part where we say whom is to disappear, when Toto came into the room and interrupted us," added Dorothy. "I said something to him like, 'You have ALL THE PALACE to play in'."

"I said, 'Yes the whole palace!'" added the Wizard. "That is the last that I remember."

"So, you two caused the trouble, but you weren't able to fix the problem!" summarized Ozma. "What am I going to do with you?"

"Perhaps you should take away our right to practice magic," suggested Dorothy.

"Not a bad idea," agreed Ozma. "However, I need the Wizard to do magic once in a while. I think I will take the Twin Book of Spells away from you."

"That might be for the best," agreed the Wizard.

"Glinda, would you take charge of the book," requested Ozma. "Once everything is straightened out, please destroy it."

"Yes Your Majesty," responded Glinda.

"Now Wizard, I understand about the reason for the repeating day. However, why did you want to make a person disappear?" questioned Ozma.

"I wanted to make people disappear and reappear," stated the Wizard. "It was my intention to use the spell to entertain guests."

"That trick is a little too dangerous to be used just to entertain guests, don't you think?" remarked Ozma.

"Yes Your Majesty," answered the Wizard.

"Dorothy, I expected you to have more sense than to be involved in this," stated Ozma. "After all, you are a Princess of Oz."

"Yes Your Majesty," agreed Dorothy.

"Now then if Dorothy and the Wizard disappeared too, how did they break the spell?" requested Ozma.

"They didn't, Your Majesty," answered Glinda. "Vicki and Don broke the spell."

"Are Don and Vicki great witches or sorcerers?" asked Ozma.

"No, we are not," replied Don.

"We are just two cousins who happen to have fun together flying balloons," insisted Vicki.

"The counter spell for the witch or sorcerer accidently making themselves disappear required the Twin Rulers of Oz must say the spell together. In fact, it must be said using Twin Talk!" announced Glinda. "That is why Vicki and Don had to become the new Rulers of Oz after your disappearance."

"So, that is why I am no longer the Ruler of Oz," remarked Ozma. "Thank you, Don and Vicki for becoming Twin Rulers of Oz."

"We just happened to drop in," insisted Vicki. "You can have your kingdom back anytime you wish."

"I will talk with you about that later," stated Ozma. "One more time, why did it take two and half weeks to undo the spell?"

"The palace was locked and we couldn't find a way in," said the Tin Woodman. "Three days ago, Don found a way into the palace. It took three more days to discover what had happened and find the counter spell."

"Good, I finally understand! Now, if you don't mind, I think I will have something to eat and get some sleep," announced Ozma. "Is it all right for me to use my old quarters?"

"Please do," insisted Don. "We never wanted to use them."

"Thank you," said Ozma. "Have a good night."

The Wizard, Glinda, Tin Woodman, Vicki, and Don bowed and started to leave Ozma's quarters.

"One more question. How do we undo this repeating day spell?" requested Vicki.

"You don't," stated the Wizard. "Dorothy and I will undo it at the stroke of midnight."

"They will wait until midnight of the day you two leave the Land of Oz," corrected Glinda.

"I don't understand. Why wait?" requested Don.

"For one thing, the counter spell only works at midnight," said the Wizard.

"For another reason, you two still have a balloon record to set," insisted Glinda. "We appreciate your help in the Land of Oz, but we don't want to interfere with your outside world activities. So, you will have to leave the Land of Oz while it is still June 20. That is of course if it is all right with Ozma."

"Of course it is fine with me," stated Ozma.

"That is very kind of you," stated Vicki and Don together.

Once again everyone wished Ozma a good night and the visitors left Ozma's quarters.

Chapter 20

Vicki and Don Abdicate Their Thrones

The next morning, a royal court session was called. It was time to welcome back all the missing persons and to decide who should be the Ruler or Rulers of Oz.

Don and Vicki were sitting on their thrones. The Tin Woodman and Glinda were on the left of the thrones. The Wizard and Scarecrow stood on the right of the thrones. The throne room was full once more with many rulers from surrounding lands and all the rulers in the Land of Oz. They were talking in small groups. They were awaiting the arrival of Ozma.

The Chamberlain rapped on the floor with his staff.

"Announcing Her Majesty, Ozma, Ex-Ruler of All Oz," cried the Chamberlain. "All bow!"

The room became silent. Every eye was on Ozma. Everyone bowed toward her.

"Please, all rise!" called Ozma, as she started walking toward the thrones. "We are all good friends."

Ozma reached the thrones, stopped and bowed to the Twin Rulers of Oz.

"I see you made some changes since I ruled Oz," remarked Ozma.

"Well, we needed two thrones as we are your Twin Rulers," stated Vicki. "I am sure that one of the thrones can be removed after you become the ruler once more."

"What if I do not choose to be Ruler of Oz again?" asked Ozma.

"I guess we will have to get the Scarecrow or the Patchwork Girl to be the ruler," suggested Vicki. "Don and I have urgent business in the outside world."

"Yes indeed!" agreed Don. "We have a balloon flight to continue. After all, we were only brought to Oz to solve the mystery of your disappearance. That mystery has been solved. There is no longer a need for us to stay in Oz."

"You didn't enjoy being Rulers of Oz?" asked Ozma.

"It has its good and bad side," remarked Don. "Frankly, being a ruler isn't as much fun as one would imagine it to be."

"You are right, cousin. We didn't get to do what we wanted to do at all," added Vicki. "It seemed like we were always being told what we had to do next."

"You didn't enjoy any of it?" requested Ozma.

"Well, the food was good," admitted Don. "And it was nice being treated like royalty."

"Of course I did get to wear some wonderful outfits," acknowledged Vicki. "I even got waited on hand and foot. I guess a few days of it were okay for something different, but now I want to go back to my own world."

"Yes. We want to get back to our record balloon flight," said Don. "We also want to stop Aunt Peggy and Uncle Robert from worrying about us."

"So, as long as you are Rulers of Oz, you can't return to your own life," summarized Ozma. "I suppose we must do something about that."

"What do we need to do?" asked Don.

"You need to abdicate your thrones," responded Ozma.

"Okay. How do we go about abdicating our thrones?" asked Vicki.

"That is fairly simple," said Ozma. "You just take off your crowns, hand them to the Tin Woodman and Scarecrow, and announce you hereby renounce your thrones."

"We wish to do that, but first we would like to know that someone will replace us and that the Land of Oz will be in good hands," insisted Don.

"This is the Land of Oz," announced Ozma. "Everything has a way of working out for the best in the end. Don't worry about it."

"You are not going to tell us who will be the next Ruler of Oz, are you?" remarked Don.

"It is not up to me to say," stated Ozma. "It is up to these folks in the throne room and all the rest of the people of the Land of Oz."

"Please don't worry about it, we can always find someone who wants to rule Oz," continued Ozma.

"Sure you can!" exclaimed Vicki. "I understand the Nome King is willing to rule Oz. I believe he is also interested in getting back an old belt."

"He tried to get the belt back, did he," remarked Oz.

"Yes he did," stated Don. "Don't worry. He didn't get it. You will find it in your quarters. Everything else of yours is right where you left it."

"See! You two did a fine job of ruling Oz," acknowledged Ozma. "Are you sure you don't want to continue to rule Oz?"

"We really do need to go back to the outside world," insisted Vicki. "Being in Oz is an experience we will never forget, but this isn't our home."

"So, we will be leaving the Land of Oz very soon," added Don.

"Okay. What must be must be!" stated Ozma. "I think it is time for your abdicating."

Vicki and Don stood up.

"We thank you for your help and loyalty," announced Don to those present..

"However, we must be going," stated Vicki. "It was nice knowing all of you."

Don and Vicki walked down from their thrones. Ozma moved off to the right of the thrones.

The Tin Woodman and Scarecrow were waiting at the bottom of the steps.

Together, Vicki and Don announced, "We hereby renounce our thrones."

Don handed his crown to the Tin Woodman. Vicki handed her crown to the Scarecrow.

"It was fun and we love you all," said Vicki, with tears in her eyes. "You treated us so wonderful!"

"But now we need to get back to our outside world business," added Don.

Everyone bowed to the Ex-Rulers of Oz.

"Now, we will just go to our quarters," announced Don.

"Not so fast," commanded Glinda. "Surely you want to see who is going to be crowned the next Ruler of Oz?"

"Well, I guess we could wait around for a few minutes. I am just a little bit curious," admitted Vicki.

Glinda ushered Vicki and Don to one side of the thrones.

"I wonder if there are to be new Twin Rulers of Oz?" remarked Don. "There are still two thrones and crowns."

"Thank you for reminding me of that," replied Glinda. "I can fix that."

She took a magic wand from her sleeve, said a short spell, and waved the wand at the two thrones. The two thrones moved toward each other until they merged into a single emerald throne.

Next she waved the wand at the two crowns held on two pillows by the Tin Man and the Scarecrow. The Scarecrow's crown and pillow moved toward the pillow and crown the Tin Woodman was holding until there was just one crown and pillow.

"If you two would move over by Ozma, the Scarecrow, and Wizard, who are also Ex-Rulers of Oz, we can get on with the coronation of the new Ruler of All Oz," requested Glinda.

"If I may have everyone's attention," called Glinda. "I would first like to remind everyone that we now have five Ex-Rulers of Oz with us today. You all know the Wizard, the Scarecrow, Ozma, Vicki, and Don."

Everyone bowed to the Ex-Rulers.

"I now call upon all of you," continued Ozma. "If any of you besides these Ex-Rulers of Oz wishes to be the new Ruler of All Oz, please come forward!"

The room grew quiet. One could have heard a pin dropped. No one moved.

"Are you sure none of you wish to be the next Ruler of the Land of Oz?" called Glinda.

This was greeted by nothing put silence.

"In that case, I now call upon the Ex-Rulers of Oz. Does any of you wish to be the next Ruler of Oz?" requested Glinda.

No one said a word.

"This is most distressing!" admitted a confused Glinda. "Ozma, I thought for sure at least one of you would offer to be the next Ruler of Oz."

"Perhaps you are asking the wrong question?" suggested Ozma.

"I don't understand," replied Glinda.

"What day is this?" requested Ozma.

"This is June 20," responded Glinda

"And what time is it?" asked Ozma.

"It is ten o'clock in the morning," replied Glinda.

"What day did Don and Vicki become Rules of Oz?"

"On June 20," stated Glinda.

"At what time did they become rulers?"

"At two o'clock in the afternoon," answered Glinda. "However, I still don't understand what you are getting at. What has the time got to do with anything?"

"It is fun to be able to confuse someone as smart as you for once," laughed Ozma. "It is very simple. You have been asking the wrong question. Think!"

"I am still lost. What question should I have been asking?" requested Glinda.

"Why you should have been asking, 'Who is the Ruler of All of Oz'," stated Ozma. "Try asking that question!"

"Okay," said a still baffled Glinda. "Who is the Rule of All of Oz?"

The room went silent once more. Finally, after a moment, Ozma announced, "I, Ozma, am the Ruler of All of Oz."

The room broke out in applause. Vicki and Don were especially loud in their applause.

"I still don't follow you," stated Glinda.

"It is very simple," insisted Ozma. "On June 20, at ten o'clock in the morning, I was still the Ruler of Oz. Don and Vicki will not become the rulers until later in the day. However, since they have advocated, I will remain the Ruler of Oz."

"You do make that sound simple," agreed Glinda. "So, we don't need a new ruler after all."

"No indeed. We don't need a new ruler," agreed the Tin Man.

The Scarecrow placed the crown on Ozma's head. She climbed up into the throne.

"All bow to the Ruler of All of Oz," shouted Don.

"Long live Ozma, Ruler of All of Oz!" added Vicki.

"Hail Ozma, Ruler of Oz!" cried the people.

Everyone bowed to Ozma.

"All rise!" commanded Ozma. "I have an announcement."

The room went silent again.

"Our honored guests and now Ex-Rulers of Oz, Vicki and Don will be leaving us later today," announced Ozma. "It seems they have pressing matters to attend to in the outside world. We all wish them a safe journey."

"Wizard, will you please help Don and Vicki check out their balloon. Also will Glinda please meet me in my quarters," continued Ozma. "We need to prepare for Don and Vicki's departure."

"I would be delighted to help Vicki and Don with checking out their balloon," replied an excited Wizard.

"Whatever you need, I am ready to help you," acknowledged Glinda.

"This audience is over. You are all dismissed!" commanded Ozma, as she rose to leave the throne room.

Everyone bowed to Ozma. Once Ozma left the room everyone else left too.

Ozma and Glinda met in Ozma's sitting room. Plans were made for Vicki and Don's departure. Messengers came and went from the sitting room.

Chapter 21

The Wizard Helps Test Drive the Balloon

"Wizard, we are ready. Let us go check out the balloon equipment," called Vicki.

"I think we should have lunch first," suggested Don.

"It is still early. Why not check out the equipment, have an early lunch, and then test flight the balloon after lunch?" offered the Wizard.

"Okay," agreed Don and Vicki in unison.

Don, Vicki, and Wizard used an open wagon to go out to the balloon just outside the Emerald City. Hank the Mule acted as the horse and Betsy Bobbin went along for the ride.

"Wow! This thing is huge!" exclaimed the Wizard, as the wagon halted next to the balloon.

The heat absorbing material was half covered, making the balloon black with white stripes. It was tugging at its tie down ropes.

While Don and Vicki had been busy being the Rulers of Oz, some of the mechanics from the Emerald City had checked over the balloon for leaks. The propane and oxygen tanks have been refilled.

The Wizard, Betsy Bobbin, Don, and Vicki were helped into the basket. It was a bit crowded. Vicki show the others all the equipment as Don explained how everything worked.

Vicki tried out the radio. She called, "Shadow Five, this is Balloon One. Can you hear me Daddy?"

All they heard from the radio was static.

Everything checked out okay.

They all returned to the palace.

The Wizard had an early lunch with Vicki and Don, in Vicki's dining room

The Wizard told Don and Vicki about his travels using a hydrogen-filled balloon. The balloon carried bags of sand. One emptied out some sand to make the balloon lighter so it would rise. To get the balloon to lose altitude, one had to let some gas out of the bag.

Don told the Wizard that their balloon uses hot air to make it rise. It used heat absorbing material to heat the air. It could also use a propane heater.

The discussion went on for twenty minutes. Finally, the Wizard asked if he could take a ride in the balloon.

"We know the balloon is repaired and restocked," remarked Vicki. "We don't need to leave here until later this afternoon. I think we should test flight the balloon. What do you think?"

"We wouldn't want to take a long flight in an untested balloon," agreed Don. "Perhaps the Wizard could help us test drive the balloon?"

"Oh, could I!" exclaimed the Wizard. "I mean I can probably find time to help you out. The other things I have to do can wait for a while."

"Good!" announced Vicki. "Let's go test out the balloon as soon as we finish lunch."

The Wizard arranged for the open wagon to be brought around. This time the Sawhorse of Oz was available to pull the wagon.

Ozma and the Tin Woodman met them at the palace entrance. When they found out that the Wizard was going for a balloon ride, they asked if they could come watch it.

Everyone got in the wagon and told the sawhorse to head for the big balloon which could just be seen over the city wall.

A few minutes later, the Sawhorse halted the wagon next to the balloon.

"As you know, the basket isn't very large," stated Don. "I think it will hold three of us if one of us sits on the ice chest."

"That will be fine," agreed the Wizard. "I will sit on the chest and try to stay out of your way."

While they prepared the balloon for flight, more people came out to watch it including Glinda, Professor Wogglebug, Button Bright, and the Shaggy Man.

Some of the people watching over the balloon helped the Wizard, Vicki and Don into the basket. A smoke rocket was set off to show how the winds were blowing.

The balloon was launched. It rose to several hundred feet before Don and Vicki got it trimmed.

They allowed it to float over the fields of blue flowers headed for Munchkin Country.

Don trimmed the balloon and allowed it to rise until they found a wind blowing back the way they had come.

A short time later, they were floating above the Emerald City, headed for Winkie Country.

Vicki adjusted the trim so that the balloon would fall back to three hundred feet and caught a wind blowing back to the Emerald City.

The Wizard was allowed to try his hand at operating the balloon. He trimmed the balloon, had it rise and fall. He even got to tryout the propane burner.

Two hours after lifting off, they landed the balloon back where they had taken off from.

"Wow! Absolutely amazing!" remarked the Wizard. He enjoyed the ride.

"So you did enjoy your ride," remarked Ozma.

"Indeed I did," responded the Wizard. "I am going to have to make me one of these balloons for myself."

"I take it the flight went okay," added the Tin Woodman.

"It went very well," answered Don. "I think we are ready to continue our flight."

"We have a few hours to wait yet," stated Ozma. "You should have a little rest before you leave."

Chapter 22

Returning to the Outside World

Don and Vicki were delivered to their balloon by a wagon drawn by the Cowardly Lion and Hungry Tiger. The balloon's propane tank had been top off and the ice chest restocked with food. The balloon was straining at the tie down ropes.

A large crowd had assembled to watch them take off, including Ozma, Glinda, the Wizard of Oz, Dorothy, Toto, Button-Bright, the Shaggy Man, the Scarecrow, the Tin Woodman, the Wooden Sawhorse, Hunk the Mule, Betsy Bobbin, Billina and her chicks, the Hungry Tiger, and the Cowardly Lion, and many, many more of their new friends. They were seeing off the Ex-Co King and Queen of the Emerald City and Oz. Everyone was wishing Vicki and Don a happy and safe journey.

Picnic tables had been set up and everyone was having a good time. Snacks, food, and drink of all kinds were available for everyone to eat.

Vicki and Don had to wait for the arrival of another guest, Polychrome the Daughter of the Rainbow King, before they could leave Oz.

Rain clouds were gathering to the south.

"We shouldn't have long to wait for our guest," remarked Ozma. "It only takes a little rain to allow a rainbow."

"Why do we need a rainbow?" asked Don.

"We need the help of the Rainbow King to get you two back to the outside world," answered Glinda. "Polychrome is the Rainbow King's daughter and will be his representative. Polychrome travels by rainbows, so we need a rainbow. Rainbows always follow the rain."

"So, what do we need to do?" requested Vicki.

"You two just need to takeoff when we tell you to and fly into the thunderstorm," stated Ozma. "Everything else will be taken care of by us."

"That all there is to it!" remarked Don. "We came to Oz by thunderstorm and we are now going home by thunderstorm."

"Well, it isn't quite that easy, but that is the general idea," agreed Glinda. "However, I would not advise you to make flying into thunderstorms a regular habit."

"Believe me. We will not do that," insisted Vicki.

"We were lucky to survive the thunderstorm flight that brought us here," added Don. "It should have destroyed the balloon."

"Just this one more time, you must fly into a thunderstorm," stated Glinda. "You will be safe. Don't worry."

A light rain started to fall. Everyone got out umbrellas in the colors of red, blue, green, yellow, and purple, depending on which region of Oz they were from. Vicki and Don took cover in the balloon gondola.

The rain stopped and a rainbow formed. It ended at the foot of the balloon. A beautiful sky fairy came dancing down the rainbow to the ground.

"Hello, Polychrome," greeted Ozma. "What a pleasure to see you again."

"It is nice to see you too, Omza and friends," said Polychrome.

"Does your father understand what we need him to do?" requested Glinda.

"Yes, he does and he has got the thunder fairies to agree to help him," stated Polychrome. "Are these the outsiders we are helping?"

"King Don and Queen Vicki, this is Polychrome," said Ozma. "They are the now Ex-Rulers of Oz."

"Hi!" called Vicki and Don together.

"Hello, Your Majesties," replied Polychrome.

"It was fun being the King and Queen of the Emerald City and Oz," said Vicki, "but we are worried about our families wondering about what has happened to us."

"Don't forget that we were trying to set a cross country balloon record," added Don. "Although I guess stopping our families from worrying is more important than any record."

"Have a little faith in me and the Land of Oz," replied Ozma. "You two have been a great help to the Land of Oz. Now, it is time the Land of Oz helped you."

"From the looks of the thunder clouds just south of here, I think it is time for everyone to say goodbye," announced Glinda.

Everyone said goodbye to one another. Polychrome danced back up the rainbow and it disappeared. The thunder clouds were very close, very black, with flashing lights in them. The lights were flashing in the colors of red, green, blue, yellow, and purple. All the magic of Oz was in the storm.

"Your Majesty," said Glinda to Ozma. "It is time!"

"Launch the balloon!" shouted Ozma.

The ground crew let go of the tie down ropes. The balloon rose slowly into the air.

Vicki and Don waved to the large crowd below them. They could see Dorothy, Toto, Ozma, the Wizard, the Tin Man, the Scarecrow, the Cowardly Lion, the Hungry Tiger, the Wooden Sawhorse, Betsy Bobbin, Hank the Mule, Billina and her chicks, Button-Bright, the Shaggy Man, and many, many more of their new friends. The crowd waved back.

The balloon rose faster. Don and Vicki adjusted the trim to slow the ascent. To their south, they could see the large thunderstorm clouds growing in size. The balloon was drifting toward the clouds. As the balloon rose higher, the air got colder. At three thousand feet, Don and Vicki put on their fur lined flight suits. They got out their gloves and helmets and connected up the oxygen equipment.

A rainbow appeared next to the balloon and Polychrome came dancing down it. She waved at Vicki and Don. She shouted at them that all was ready. All they had to do was sit back and enjoy the ride.

Polychrome and the rainbow disappeared. The crowd on the ground could no longer be seen by Don and Vicki.

The sound of thunder was heard. The lightening flashed. The balloon rose higher. By the time the balloon had reach seven thousand feet, it had entered the storm.

The balloon rose faster. Vicki and Don trimmed the heat absorbing material to stop the rise of the balloon. Of course the balloon just kept following the up drafts.

Soon the balloon was above ten thousand feet. The oxygen equipment was turned on and the intercom connected. The balloon continued to rise.

Don set an alarm to let them know when the balloon dropped below ten thousand feet.

The balloon rose. The lightening flashed. The thunder roared. The balloon basket rocked back and forth.

Don and Vicki were sitting in the bottom of the basket waiting for the movement to stop. Time passed slowly. The oxygen ran out and both of them fell asleep.

Chapter 23

The Balloon is found

"Shadow Five, this is Phoenix air traffic control," crackled the radio next to Robert. "We have a large blip at twelve thousand feet above Fort Apache. The object is descending at 500 feet per minute. It is drafting east at thirty knots. It is either the missing balloon or a very large and slow UFO. It seems to be at the east edge of the storm."

"This is the traffic control supervisor," said another voice. "What is this about an UFO?"

"It is not a UFO, sir," stated the air traffic controller. "It is Balloon One. Shadow Five, if you turn to a new heading of 045 degrees magnetic, you should interrupt it in ten minutes."

"This is Shadow Five. We are headed toward Fort Apache from the east," replied Robert. "We will change course to 045 degrees magnetic. If they continue their rate of descent we should catch up with them in about ten minutes at 7,000 feet. Thank you."

"This is Phoenix air traffic control. We will continue to track the balloon and give you updates."

"Balloon One ground crew, this is Shadow Five," said Robert into the radio. "Have you been listening to my conversation with Phoenix air traffic control?"

"Shadow Five, this is the Ground Crew," responded the radio. "Yes we have."

"Please head east from Fort Apache. The balloon is bypassing you," stated Robert. "We will give you more directions later."

Frank and Robert headed for Fort Apache. They could see the storm clouds but not the balloon. Once they got near the clouds, they started circling around just outside the clouds.

"Phoenix air traffic control, do you still have the balloon on radar?" requested Robert.

From the radio came a reply, "Yes, Shadow Five, we have the balloon at the edge of the storm, just east of Fort Apache. It is now at ten thousand feet and descending. You should be able to see it anytime now."

"Thank you, Phoenix air traffic control," said Robert. "We will let you know when we see it."

Robert and Frank continued to on their course. For several more minutes, they saw nothing but clouds.

Suddenly, Robert saw the black and white balloon emerge from the clouds below them.

"Phoenix, this is Shadow Five. We see the balloon below us. It is between eight and nine thousand feet," announced Robert into the radio.

"That is good news, Shadow Five," answered the radio. "We just lost the balloon as it went below nine thousand feet."

"Shadow Five this is Balloon One. Is that you Daddy?" called Vicki.

"Balloon One this is Shadow Five. Yes, this is your father. Are you all right?"

"We are busy trying to land. Otherwise, we are okay," replied the radio. "There seems to be a road just east of us. We will try to land near it."

"That sounds very well. We will try to get hold of the ground crew and keep an eye on you," stated Robert.

"Balloon One ground crew, this is Shadow Five. Do you read me over?" called Robert.

"Shadow Five, this is Balloon One ground crew," said a voice on the radio. "Where are you?"

"I think we are about fifty miles east of Fort Apache," answered Robert. "I think that would put us near highway 77, between Show Low and Snowflake."

"Between Show Low and Snowflake on highway 77," repeated the radio. "Where do people get names like that for towns?"

"I don't know where the names came from, but those are the names of the towns. How soon can you reach them?" requested Robert

"We are just approaching Show Low. We will turn left and head for Snowflake. It should only be a few minutes before we see you," came the radio replied.

"Don and Vicki, how is the landing coming?" asked Robert.

"We are about one hundred feet above the ground," answered Vicki. "We should be dropping our anchor shortly."

"We will circle until the ground crew reaches you."

"Thank you, Uncle," called Don. "I am dropping the anchor. Hang on."

A few seconds later, the anchor dragged along the ground seeking something to grab hold of. Finally, it got stuck between two boulders. The basket tipped over as the slack in the rope was taken up. Finally the balloon halted.

"Daddy, we have landed," announced Vicki. "We have tipped over, but are all right."

"That is good news!" stated Robert. "Stay with the balloon. The ground crew has almost reached you."

Several minutes later, the radio called, "Shadow Five, this is the ground crew. We see the balloon. We are only a couple of minutes away."

"This is Shadow Five, to Balloon One," announced Robert. "We are leaving you now. The ground crew is arriving."

"Bye, Uncle. Bye Daddy," answered the radio.

The ground crew drove up to the balloon. They were followed by a recreational vehicle. The ground crew found and tied down the ropes that held the balloon to the ground. They got out a large tank of propane, connected it to the balloon's burner, and heated the air in the balloon until it lifted the balloon and basket into an upright position.

Don and Vicki were taken inside the recreational vehicle and allowed to relax.

Portable flood lights were placed around the balloon. The heat absorbing panels were turned on full. Other servicing was done to the balloon including giving it a new oxygen tank, refilling the propane tank, and restocking the ice chest.

Vicki and Don were able to shower and have a hot meal.

Just as they finished eating, Robert joined them.

"Well, that was some balloon ride you had," stated Robert. "It seems you managed to travel about fifty miles further then we plan for today's trip."

"Does that include all the up and down traveling we did?" asked Vicki.

"No!" admitted Robert. "I guess you did go higher than we planned. They tell me you used up all your oxygen and propane."

"You wouldn't believe how far we actually traveled," added Don.

"Well, you did about 430 miles in fourteen hours," said Robert. "I think we should take it easier tomorrow."

"But we went all the way to the Land of Oz, where Don and I were rulers for several days," replied Vicki.

"You just imagined that," said Robert. "You just think you went to Oz because of being without Oxygen for a while. You will feel better after you rest."

"I seem to have imagined the same thing," added Don.

"That is just the after effects of lack of oxygen," announced Robert. "Just don't mention it to anyone else."

Just then, a member of the ground crew came into the vehicle, carrying a carton of ice cream. She reported that the balloon was in good condition and ready for tomorrow's flight. The landing had only scratched the side of the basket. The bag of the balloon was still in good shape."

"I didn't know you folks had ice cream in your ice chest," said the crew member.

"They didn't have any ice cream," insisted Robert. "I personally packed their ice chest."

"Well, we found this carton of green ice cream in the ice chest, and it is delicious!" continued the crew member.

"Please feel free to help yourself to the ice cream," suggested Don.

"Yes. That is Emerald City Ice Cream, made from green cream," stated Vicki. "It is made in the Emerald City."

"When did you sneak ice cream into the ice chest?" asked Robert.

"When we stopped to resupply the balloon in Oz," replied Don. "We stopped at the Emerald City."

"But that is just an imaginary place," stated Robert.

"So, have some imaginary ice cream," offered Vicki. She got spoons out a drawer and gave them to Robert and the crew member.

Robert tasted the ice cream. "This is good!"

"However," continued Robert. "No mention of this ice cream or your visiting Oz is to leave this room!"

"Yes, Daddy," agreed Vicki.

"Your Majesty, Vicki," said Don, "I believe your sleeping chambers are ready."

"Very good Your Majesty, Don," replied Vicki. "I believe I will now retire."

Don and Vicki headed for the sleeping quarters.

Just as they left the room, Don called over his shoulder, "Uncle, you should check with Bud and Fran about how many gun salute we got over the Chocolate Maintain Gunnery Range."

"Good night, Uncle."

"Good night Daddy."

"Good night Vicki and Don," replied Robert.

"I wonder what Don meant about a gun salute?" questioned Robert of no one in particular.

"Haven't you heard?" asked the crew member. "Bud and Fran said that they got a twenty-one gun salute when they flew over the Chocolate Maintain Gunnery Range. That salute is reserved for rulers of countries."

"Right!" agreed Robert. "That is a likely story. I think we are both tired. Let's get some sleep."

The ground crew member said goodnight to Robert and left.

Robert just shook his head when he thought over the story of Don and Vicki visiting Oz. Their being rulers of any country was just too unbelievable to be considered. The twenty-one gun salute could have been a mistake or Bud and Fran could have miscounted the number of shots. The ice cream on the other land was much harder to explain.

Finally Robert gave up the problem and went to bed.

*   *   *

Meanwhile back in the Land of Oz.

Once the balloon had entered the thunderstorm, Dorothy, the Wizard, and Glinda had the Sawhorse hitched up to the little wagon. They got in the wagon and told the Sawhorse to head to Glinda's Castle with the best possible speed.

Now the Sawhorse can pull the wagon so fast that it could take away one's breathe. Even so, the trip lasted until just before midnight.

Dorothy, the Wizard, and Glinda went to in Glinda's quarters. There they opened the Twin Book of Spells to the counter spell for the repeating day spell.

At the first stroke of midnight, the Wizard and Dorothy recited the counter spell.

Immediately there after, Glinda looked in her Great Book of Records to see what day it was. The book showed the date as June 21!

Glinda took the Twin Book of Spells from the Wizard. She set it in the fireplace, pulled out her magic wand and said a few magic words. The book burst into flames and was destroyed!

"I am sure we will all be better off knowing that Mombi's old magic book has been destroyed!" announced Glinda. "You two do agree with me, don't you?"

"Yes!" replied the Wizard. "We most certainly do!"

"We thought it was safe to use it, but I guess we were wrong!" added Dorothy.

"Next time you find something of Old Mombi's, take it to Ozma," commanded Glinda.

"We will!" the Wizard assured her.

"Absolutely!" agreed Dorothy.

The Wizard and Dorothy bowed and left Glinda's presence. They were ashamed of themselves for all the trouble they had caused.

Even though all was forgiven, it took a few days before Dorothy and the Wizard were back in good standing with Ozma and Glinda.

Toto, Dorothy and the Wizard were careful not to practice any more unauthorized magic.

The calendar in Oz was once more advancing as it should. No more people disappeared from the palace or anywhere else in Oz.

X – Thunderstrom

Chapter 24

The Balloon Flight Continues

By the next morning, everyone had forgotten about Don and Vicki saying they had visited the Land of Oz. It even seemed like a dream to Vicki and Don.

At dawn the next morning, the balloon was launched to continue the flight across the country.

It took fourteen more days to complete the trip to New York, New York. They could have done it in twelve days but they laid over a day in Tennessee and another day in Virginia to miss flying in thunderstorms.

The fight didn't take them through any more storms. In fact, nothing at all exciting happened during those fourteen days, except they got to see a large bit of the United States. The view of the Mississippi river was worth the trip. The New York skyline is much more impressive from a hot air balloon than from the ground. During the trip, Don and Vicki had gotten to see from sea to sea (Pacific to Atlantic), the desert, the mountains, and the plains. The flight crossed the Chesapeake Bay. The balloon had passed over the twelve states of: California, Arizona, New Mexico, Texas,

Oklahoma, Arkansas, Tennessee, Virginia, Maryland, Delaware, New Jersey, and New York.

Everything had gone well until they reached New York City. There were a few scary minutes when several news helicopters got too close to the balloon in New York City. The news services were competing with each other over who could get the closest shot of Don and Vicki. The result was that the balloon was buffeted about and did spill out some of its hot air. The helicopters only backed off when Robert threatened to ram them.

Even so, the balloon dropped more than one hundred feet before Don and Vicki got the propane burner going. They got a closer look at some of the skyscrapers than was intended.

The record setting balloon flight ended when Don and Vicki set the balloon down in the middle of Central Park.

A huge crowd was waiting to greet them. Aunt Peggy was in the front of the crowd.

Aunt Peggy had flown out to see Don and Vicki's landing in Central Park.

Vicki and Don did set the record for the fastest hot air balloon flight across the country using just hot air. They were also the youngest pilots to do so.

Of course Malcolm Forbes still held the record for being the first person to do it in a hot air balloon.

Other trans-America balloon flights had been faster, but they used a combination of helium and hot air, but Don and Vicki were the fastest ones using just hot air in the balloon.

New York welcomed them with a ticker tape parade. Vicki and Don were given the key to the city. They visited many of the famous places and stores in the New York area. You could even say they were treated like royalty!

Don and Vicki got to go on many of the talk shows. They had a great visit in New York.

Both Vicki's and Don's parents were very proud of their children.

By the time all the excitement had died away, Don and Vicki could hardly remember their trip to Oz. It all seemed like a long ago dream.

The return flight to San Diego was by airplane. It only took five hours.

Will Vicki and Don ever visit the Land of Oz again?

If so, will they rule Oz once more?

Only time will tell.

FROM THIS POINT ON OCTOBER 4, 1973
MALCOLM FORBES OF NEW YORK BEGAN
THE FIRST TRANSCONTINENTAL CROSSING
OF THE UNITED STATES IN A HOT AIR
BALLOON. HIS UNIQUE JOURNEY ENDED
ON NOVEMbER 5, 1973, IN CHESAPEAKE
BAY NEAR NEWPORT NEWS, VIRGINIA.

Afterward

I wrote the draft of Don and Vicki Co-Rulers of Oz while I lived in Ontario, Oregon. It is fifty miles north-east of Boise, Idaho. Shortly thereafter, my wife and I were on vacation on the coast of Oregon. We found the above sign in the picnic area of Sunset Beach State Park.

The first transcontinental hot air balloon crossing of the United States was done in 1973 and took just over a month to complete. It was done by Malcolm Forbes and started at Sunset Beach State Park, near Charleston, Oregon; and ended in the Chesapeake Bay near Newport News, Virginia,

The fill story of the flight can be found on the Web at:

www.lighterthanair.org/ellis/ed_yost.htm

You want to read that section on: The Forbes Transcontinental Balloon.

Forbes planned to start the flight from San Diego in July, but Yost told him that the summer thunderstorms would kill him. Yost talked him into taking off from near Coos Bay, Oregon, instead. That probably was a good decision by Malcolm.